Meant to Bee

MEANT TO BEE

For information, contact: http://www.stormshultz.com

Cover design by Kelsey Gietl.

Editing by Heather Wood.

ISBN: 979-8-9866147-0-0

Meant to Bee

A sweet romantic comedy

Storm Shultz

For those of you who wish to run away
and own a small English cottage and a goat.
And for my sweet husband, who isn't convinced that owning a cottage with a goat is a real dream goal. One day, babe, one day.

Chapter One
Cordy

The overpowering smell of fish claws at my nostrils, making it hard to concentrate on the woman in front of me.

"Name?" She snaps her gum without looking up.

"Cordelia Brown." My voice sounds dry even to my own ears. I try to pep it up by adding, "But I go by Cordy."

"There's no place to indicate preferred names." The woman still doesn't look up from her form.

"Oh, okay. Never mind then." I lean back in my seat to get away from the tuna on her breath. From my new vantage point, I can now see the half-eaten and discarded sandwich in the trashcan next to her desk.

I sit in silence and wait for the woman to carefully write out my name. This is quite possibly the dreariest employment office I've ever been in. There are no windows, and although the English sky is mostly overcast, it would help to at least be able to see something of nature.

The whole office is also stuck in the sixties, which is one of my least favorite decades. Everyone is filling everything out on paper, the walls are cigarette smoke-stained, and the only computers in the room are the biggest, boxiest looking things I've ever seen. Even the woman sitting in front of me—I've already forgotten her name—has a hairstyle straight out of the sixties.

I scan the desk in front of me, looking for the name plaque of the woman who is helping to keep me and my daughter from starving.

Sydney Waterford.

She looks like a Sydney Waterford.

Sydney Waterford looks back up at me. She's in her late fifties, which means she was probably born in the sixties and has no excuse for having such an outdated hairstyle.

Stop it, Cordy. Maybe she likes her hair like that. Maybe it makes her happy. Her hair is not hurting you.

"Any dependents?"

I sit up in my chair. "Yes, I have a daughter."

"How old?"

"Ten months." I'm tempted to tell her how excited I am for Poppy's birthday, but she doesn't look like she cares.

"And what does your husband do?" Sydney Waterford doesn't glance up from the form, where her pen is poised over the next line.

"I don't have a husband."

Finally, she looks up. "No husband?"

"No."

She squints. "A wife?"

"How very progressive of you," I say, my tone a bit more sarcastic than I mean for it to be. "No. No husband, no wife, no boyfriend or girlfriend. No partner at all, in fact. I'm a single mom."

Sydney Waterford doesn't look as if she approves of this. Her lips have gone flat, and she even gives her head a minuscule shake as she begins writing again. I can feel irritation flaring up inside of me. This has been the longest week of my life, and I don't feel like getting attitude from someone who has her hair teased into a foot-high beehive.

"Look, what do you want from me?" The words come out sharp and loud in the small space. Tears are already pricking my eyes. "That little girl is the best thing to ever happen to me."

The two other sleepy employees look up from their desks in surprise. This room is too small for me to be shouting, but I'm so tired of people acting as if Poppy is a problem.

I'm breathing hard, but mostly because I'm trying not to cry. It's not this woman's fault she's surprised about my little family. I'm just so tired. Especially after the week I've had.

Sydney Waterford looks shocked. "I'm . . . I'm sorry, ma'am, I wasn't—" she sputters.

I can see on her face that she didn't mean to upset me. I try to relax back into my chair.

"I'm sorry, I shouldn't have shouted."

Sydney Waterford looks like she may cry. "I have a lot of respect for single mums."

Not sure what to say, I just nod. I almost want to unload onto this poor woman about my week. Well, about my month, but that seems cruel.

Last month, I found out the super cool online job I'd had since graduating college was going bankrupt. I had been a virtual assistant for a Dutch company that claimed to be doing well. Turns out, they weren't.

Since they were bankrupt, they couldn't offer me a severance package, which meant one day I had money coming in, literally the next day I was about to be homeless. Because—and this may be a shock to you—landlords still charge rent, no matter if you can pay or not.

Then, like a naïve fool, I took all the money I had left and went house shopping. I guess I thought if I owned a house, at least Poppy and I would have somewhere to go. Which is a fine plan, except I did all my house shopping online. Houses are basically a million dollars in London, which is where we lived, so I looked at homes out in the country.

I didn't want to spare the money to take the train down to tour houses, especially if I wasn't going to like any of them. In an attempt to be frugal, I called the estate agent and asked if he could give me a tour over video chat. He agreed, but then at the last minute, I got a call saying my agent was visiting family in the States. The solution was to send me a video recording of the place.

The thing is, the video was amazing. A beautiful little cottage with climbing flowers going up the sides and a thatched roof. It even had a little picket fence covered with pink flowers. Who doesn't want to live in a fairytale cottage?

So I signed the paperwork over the phone, had the keys mailed to me while I packed up our stuff, sold what I didn't want to deal with, and finally made the move.

Except, the video of the house must have been at least two years old. When Poppy and I arrived, we found the roof had visible gaps from the outside, there were rock-shaped holes in most of the windows, half of the fence was knocked down, and there wasn't a single flower in sight.

We moved in three days ago, and I haven't been able to stop crying. Not in front of Poppy, of course, but after she goes to sleep. The worst part is, I don't have enough money to fix the roof or the windows, so there are bowls all over the house—because England happens to be the wettest place on earth short of the actual rain forest—and plastic bags taped to the windows.

But I can't unload all that onto Sydney Waterford. I can't tell her how much I need a job, and if I don't get a job soon, I may end up fishing bats out of my daughter's crib. It wouldn't help, and I've already been embarrassing enough today.

We fill out the rest of my forms in relative silence. Sydney Waterford promises to call me as soon as there is news, and I leave, feeling only a little panicked. I've done what I can. Besides canvassing the teeny town of Arbury and physically asking people for a job. Which I'm not above doing, by the way.

There are only a few businesses in Arbury. There's a general store (they're not hiring, I've already checked), the employment office (that probably should have told me something), a café, the town museum, a church, and what looks like a regular house that has a plaque in the window promising it to be the city council.

If people don't work at one of these small places, they drive the two hours to London (miserable) or work from their homes. For example, there's a woman who lives three streets up from me who runs a mini daycare in her home, which is where Poppy is right now. She promised to charge me only half price since I'm out job hunting. It's the kindest anyone has been to me in what feels like a very long time. She could have made me pay full price, and then I'd have to figure out how to buy dinner for the rest of the week.

I do have an extra few pounds that turned up in my jeans pocket the last time I did laundry, and given how awful the last month has been, I think I deserve a cappuccino. Letting my craving lead my footsteps, I head to the Bluebell Café.

It's a nice little café in the center of town. Flowers in old tin watering cans line the steps that lead to the yellow door. Inside the shop, there's a small display case with some cakes, muffins, and random loaves of bread.

The middle-aged woman behind the counter smiles at me as I order my small vanilla cappuccino. I would prefer hazelnut, but they only offer vanilla or mocha. Then I take a seat at one of the four tables.

I really should get Poppy and go home. I might be able to bargain a little more of a discount if I get her now, but I need to cheer up before I get her. I don't want Poppy to start picking up on my whole 'I'm-a-sad-sap-with-no-job-and-scared-I'll-starve' vibe.

I sip my cappuccino and try to formulate a plan. I don't have Wi-Fi at my home yet, so an online job like the one I had isn't likely. Also, I'm not sure I want to do a remote job again. What if the same thing happens and the company goes bankrupt? I mean, I'm sure that's unlikely, but how unlikely?

Staring into the thin coffee in front of me, I can't help but think about my mom. She wants me to come home to the States so badly. When I told her I lost my job, she was actually excited.

"You'll finally be able to come home," she chirped.

Mom has never understood that even if being in the UK hasn't been easy, England is where I want to be. I've always loved England, ever since I found out there were people, places, languages, and cultures outside my own neighborhood. While other girls in my grade were obsessed with France, dreaming of Paris nights and French accents, I was looking up jobs in Manchester and London. I would spend hours looking at pictures of quaint English cottages and farms, daydreaming that my mom would sweep me off to an all-girls English boarding school.

At fifteen, I discovered you could go to college in almost any country you wanted to. I began saving up and trying hard to have perfect grades. I wanted scholarships and money for a plane ticket so badly. It was hard and at times exhausting, which didn't help how my mom felt about my dream. She wanted me to have a fun childhood, which to her didn't mean studying all the time.

Mom wasn't exactly wrong, though. Studying is hardly any fun, especially if you don't care about the class you're taking. (Here's looking at you, math.)

But it worked. I enrolled at King's College the semester after graduating high school. I had enough money for the plane ticket there, plus room and board for two years. The scholarships covered the rest. That was five years ago, and I haven't been in the States since.

In my junior year, I met Poppy's father. He seemed like a pretty cool guy. Smart, funny, and into slightly-nerdy English majors like me. We'd been dating for over a year when I found out about Poppy.

Honestly, I had thought maybe we could have a small wedding over winter break and then in the spring welcome a baby into our lives. Apparently, I was the only one who thought that, because as soon as I told him, he disappeared. Like, actually disappeared.

I told him over the phone because I couldn't wait to tell him in person. I always wanted to be a mom, so I never thought of it as a big problem. A difficult transition, maybe. A hard last semester before I graduated, sure. But not a disaster.

He got off the phone almost as soon as I told him, and then literally vanished. He wouldn't return my calls, and when I started going by his classes to try to talk to him, one of his friends awkwardly told me he'd transferred to a different university.

I mean . . . who transfers universities?

It didn't take me long to decide he wasn't worth it and I would do it all myself. And by "it," I mean everything. Prenatal appointments, looking for apartments (because you can't live in a college dorm with a baby), budgeting, buying baby gear, thinking about names, all of it.

Luckily, my old roommate helped me find a job, and it was pretty smooth from there. Being able to work from home solved my daycare problem, and on my off days, I spent time taking Poppy to baby yoga. I never really clicked with any of the other moms, and while there were some very lonely moments, days, and nights, waking up to Poppy's face made it all worth it.

My mom has never understood why I want to stay in England. It's not that I don't love my mom or my home state of South Carolina, it's just that I want so badly to make it. I want to be here. Even with a leaky roof and a possible bat infestation. I *want* this to work.

"All right, love?"

I look up and realize I've been staring at my cup for who-knows-how-long.

"I'm okay. Sorry, I'll get going." I stand and look for somewhere to put my cup.

The woman holds out a hand for it, giving me a sympathetic smile. I hand her the half-drunk coffee.

"You wouldn't happen to be hiring, would you?" Besides me, the café is empty, and something tells me there is no need for an extra pair of hands.

"No, dear, I'm sorry." She offers me another sympathetic smile.

"Well, thanks anyway." I give a little wave as I leave.

Maybe I will have to throw in the towel and move back to live with my mom.

"Wait." I look over my shoulder at the woman who has grabbed a small notepad and is writing something down. "I'm not hiring, but Jack Nelson is looking for help on his farm, if you don't mind that kind of work."

"I don't mind *any* kind of work," I say, a little too excitedly.

"Well, here's his number." She tears the little sheet of paper and hands it to me. "His farm is on the edge of town, heading toward the main highway. He wouldn't mind if you dropped by and offered to work."

"Thank you." I smile gratefully at her. I've never worked on a farm before, but if Jack Nelson will pay enough for me to have regular food and maybe some new shoes, I will figure it out.

I half run to the Nelson farm. There is no way I'm letting this job slip away.

There's no one in the farmyard when I finally come to a stop next to the sign that reads *Nelson Farm.* A few chickens come around the corner of the small house, clucking and pecking at the ground. They watch me with beady eyes as I take a moment to catch my breath. I was never much of a runner. I'm about to go to the house and knock on the door when I see a young man come out of the barn.

I head toward him, plastering a smile on my face. I have no idea why I'm nervous. Maybe because this is a weird way to get a job. I don't normally ambush people at their homes looking for money. And let's face it, that's basically what's happening.

"Hi, Jack Nelson?" I call out.

The man looks up in surprise. He's a bit younger than me, as if he recently graduated high school. He's short and somewhat stocky and has chickenpox scars on both cheeks, but he's not unattractive.

"Hi, I'm Cordy Brown. I heard you're hiring." I'm still a little breathless when I reach him.

"I'm not Jack." His heavy accent isn't the average English lilt. It's thick and rolling, but I can't quite place it.

"Oh, sorry. Do you know where he is?" I glance into the barn, hoping to see the elusive farmer.

The guy—he looks like a high schooler, now that I'm up close—eyes me. I remember I'm in my dress slacks, a blouse, and sensible pumps. Not exactly farm attire.

"I know I'm not farm dressed, but I was out job hunting. I heard Jack needs a hand, so I wanted to come over and introduce myself. I'll be in farm clothes the next time." I smile at him.

He doesn't smile back.

I try again. "What did you say your name was?"

"I didn't. I'm Corwynn."

"Hi, Corwynn. Do you know where Jack is?"

Corwynn glares at me for a moment. "I'm looking for him as well."

I'm about to ask him why when a voice calls out. "Hello!"

We both turn to see a man in his early sixties coming out of the house. He waves cheerfully as he approaches.

"I'm Jack. What can I do for you?"

I like the look of this man. He looks a bit like Santa, rounded in the middle, with rosy cheeks. He's missing the beard, though.

"Hi, Jack. I'm Cordy Brown." I stick out a hand for him to shake.

Corwynn's voice cuts through my introduction. "I'm here about the job."

I turn to him, my mouth falling open, my outstretched hand to Jack forgotten.

"Are you?" Jack appraises Corwynn, who admittedly looks much more capable of farm work than I do.

"So am I," I say, a tad shrilly.

"You?" Jack sounds taken aback.

I really should have changed before coming here. Although if I had changed, I would have been later than Corwynn and would have missed my opportunity.

"Yes." I press forward. "I'm a hard worker, I'm always on time, and I'm a fast learner."

"You're dressed more for office work, love," Jack says, not unkindly.

"I only just heard you were hiring. I didn't want to waste time going home to change and miss out on the job." I shoot Corwynn a dark look.

Jack looks at Corwynn. "And what about you, lad?"

"I can lift three times as much as her, and I already know how to drive heavy machinery," Corwynn says flatly.

Oh my gosh. I'm about to lose this job. To some guy who doesn't even know how to smile.

"I have a daughter," I blurt out.

Both of them look confused.

"I need a job. I have to feed her." Okay, that makes me sound desperate. Mom would send me money if I need it, but I *really* don't want to ask her for money. It'll prove I can't do it, and she'll nag me even more about moving back to South Carolina.

Jack's forehead creases with worry. "Ma'am—"

"Cordy."

"Cordy." Jack nods. "Listen, Cordy, love. This is hard work. Lots of lifting and running after cows and pigs. I can't do it anymore, and I need help, but I need help from someone who will be able to throw hay bales up into the loft." He points to the upper level of the barn we're standing next to.

I can feel tears pricking at the back of my eyes. "I could learn," I gasp out. But the truth is, I don't even want to do that. It sounds awful.

Am I that desperate? I mean, I just filled out forms at the employment office five seconds ago. Maybe Sydney Waterford will call me tomorrow with a lovely little job in a supermarket, somewhere indoors where I don't have to throw hay bales that weigh almost as much as I do into the upstairs of a barn.

I can tell Jack sees my resolve crack. He puts a comforting hand on my shoulder and squeezes.

"I'm sorry, lass, but I think I'll have to give the job to this lad." He tips his head toward Corwynn, who to his credit, looks a little less stony.

I nod. "Yeah, okay."

"If I hear of any other jobs, I'll let them know you're looking." Jack pats my shoulder and drops his hand.

I can only nod again before turning and walking back to the road. There's not much more to do but pick up Poppy and go home to my swamp of a house. And wait to see if the employment office calls.

Chapter Two
Cordy

The employment office doesn't call. It's only the next day, and it's only eight in the morning, but I was hoping.

I had a long night trying to soothe Poppy because as it turns out, moving to a new home with a leaky roof isn't the best for keeping a baby happy. Thankfully, she's conked out on my bed at this moment, which allows me to go downstairs and make some coffee.

That is, it's coffee insomuch that I make coffee, but then add enough cream and sugar to turn it a lovely shade only a tad darker than my skin. So really, it's milk with a splash of coffee.

It's stopped raining, and a weak sun peeks out from behind the clouds. The leaking has even stopped. Well, except for the leak in the bathroom. I can hear the *plink plink* of water still dripping from where I'm standing in the kitchen.

If it weren't for the leaking and broken windows, this house would be gorgeous. Exposed beams run across the ceiling, giving the home a very rustic yet romantic feel. I can picture hanging copper pots and pans from the beams in the kitchen and maybe even using them to dry herbs.

Not that I have any herbs to dry. I have a teeny yard I've already daydreamed about planting stuff in, but I need a job before I go growing lavender and rosemary.

The kitchen faces the backyard, and there is a large window next to the door that leads outside. If I had a plushy loveseat, this would be the perfect place to set it so I could look outside and have coffee in the morning.

To get to the front door, I have to pass through the kitchen, past the stairs that lead up to three small bedrooms, and out through a spacious room that I'm guessing is a living room. The bathroom is off of the kitchen in its own small alcove. The kitchen is the best part, though. It's quite large and doubles as the dining area with lots of nooks and crannies just waiting to be filled with plants and furniture.

Overall, with some love, time, and money, it could be amazing.

I daydream about what color I would paint the kitchen when there's a knock on the front door. My immediate thought is that it's Jack Nelson coming to tell me he's found a job for me, but that seems very unlikely.

And sure enough, it's not Jack standing outside my front door, but instead a large man in blue workman's overalls. He has a name tag that reads *Oscar* in white lettering. Behind Oscar, parked on the street, is a large truck.

"Hello, ma'am," Oscar says in the same country burr as Sydney Waterford and Jack's. "I've got a delivery here for you."

He holds out a clipboard. I stare at it, then at him.

Folding my arms tightly, I shake my head. "I haven't ordered anything."

Oscar pulls the form back to read it, then holds it up to me, tapping a massive finger at the top of the paper. "That's your address, isn't it?"

Peering under his finger, I see that it is and reluctantly nod. "Yes, but I didn't order anything."

"Well, it's your lucky day then, isn't it?" Oscar continues to offer me the clipboard.

I frown at him. "I can't just take something that doesn't belong to me. Someone could have put down the wrong address."

He doesn't look like he cares. I push on. "What is it, anyway?"

"Bees."

"What? Bees? Like . . . like, real bees?" I stare at the truck, which doesn't look like it's housing bees, but you never know.

Oscar sighs and looks again at the clipboard in his hand. "Yeah, says here, 'Western Honeybees, four hives.'"

"Look." My chest tightens with panic. "I can't have bees. I don't know anything about bees, and I *didn't order them.*"

Okay. Oscar looks thoroughly irritated now. He finally drops the paperwork he's been trying to get me to sign, but instead of walking back to his truck, he folds his arms.

"I'll give you ten minutes to see if one of your neighbors ordered a bunch of bees, but I'm telling you, lady, these bees are *not* coming back with me."

"Wait." I hurry back inside, grab the baby monitor, and tug on the new rain boots I bought right before moving out here.

Oscar waits semi-patiently as I hurry to the house directly next to mine. I knock, but no one answers. I don't see a car in the driveway, so I hurry to the next house. There's no answer.

"Are you kidding me?" I run back to my side of the street and to the house on the left side of my place.

I know most people are probably at work, but if someone ordered four hives of bees, why didn't they wait for them to be delivered?

I knock on the third house, a tad harder than I want, almost banging on the door. After ten seconds, I'm about to go to the next house when the door opens. A surge of relief floods through me and then is immediately quenched when I look at the person who answered.

The woman shuffling onto her top step is probably in her eighties. Her glasses are at least an inch thick. There's no way she's a beekeeper.

"Ma'am, I'm sorry to bother you." I'm panting a little. "I live right there and someone in this neighborhood has ordered honeybees, but they've been delivered to my house by mistake. Do you know who could have ordered them?"

The woman blinks. "What is it, love? Bees?"

"Yes, honeybees!" I raise my voice in case she's hard of hearing.

The woman frowns. "I didn't buy no bees."

"Well, do you know who did?"

She shakes her head. "No. No one on this road would want bees."

I want to ask if she's sure, but I somehow doubt she would be up to date on who wants what. So I thank her and hurry back to the lorry driver.

He frowns at me. "Well?"

"I can't find the owners."

"Well, looks like you're about to get some bees then, aren't you." It's a statement, not a question.

Wordlessly, I stand back and let the driver unload the hives. They're square and look more like drawers stacked on each other than they do beehives.

"Here you go." Oscar snaps the door of the truck shut. "You can post signs up around the place that you've got the bees and someone may come by and get them," he adds, apparently feeling bad for foisting a bunch of bugs off on some woman in the middle of nowhere.

"Right. Thanks."

Oscar hands the paperwork over, and this time I take it and sign my name at the bottom. There's no name on the form, just my as-of-three-days-ago address. Great.

Oscar's left the hives in a neat row next to the small, broken picket fence in my front yard. I wish I'd asked him to carry them to the backyard, but if I do find whose bees they are, they'll have to come get them, and the front yard is easier to load them back up.

The strange thing is, the hives aren't doing anything. I don't hear buzzing, and I don't even see one bee. I'm tempted to look more closely at them, but I also don't want to spook the bees and risk getting stung.

Instead of investigating the possibly empty hives (should I try to wave down Oscar and tell him to be on the lookout for bees in his truck?), I hurry back inside to get dressed. Once Poppy wakes up, I'll walk around town and try to find the rightful owner of the bees. Besides, someone could be hiring that I haven't thought of yet.

By the time I've gotten dressed, I can see Poppy on my BabyCam coming to. She started walking last week and has been exercising this new skill as much as she can. Since she's on my bed, I hurry upstairs to get her before she falls off.

"Hi, baby," I coo as I step into the room. Poppy's eyes are already open, and she turns to beam at me. My heart immediately swells at the sight of her, and I can feel a bit of the tension in my body ease.

I get her changed and dressed at record speed, then take her to the kitchen for some breakfast. As the oatmeal cools, I hurry around and pack everything I will need into Poppy's diaper bag. I bought the bag back when I had a steady income, and it's a pretty pale lavender faux leather. It can be worn as a backpack and is buttery smooth. It's one of the nicest things I own now.

I pack everything up into Poppy's stroller—another item that is too nice for my current living conditions—then set Poppy in. She babbles cheerfully, throwing in random "mamas" and "gos," which are the only words she knows so far. Handing her the stuffed pony she adores, I buckle her firmly into her stroller.

"Mama, go!" she finally chirps, and I laugh and kiss her head.

"Yes, baby, we're going."

We spend the next two hours going up to doors and into the few places people congregate, asking if anyone has ordered bees. No one has. It's the most frustrating day of my life.

Well, besides the day I realized I was being fired with no severance pay.

At last, we end up at the Bluebell Café, which has a few customers when Poppy and I trundle up. An elderly couple sits at the table by the window, both silently gazing out into the street, and a boy in his early teens is buying a pastry at the counter.

The same woman who sold me my coffee yesterday is working again. It's likely she's the only employee, and maybe even the owner, I realize. She smiles when I enter, and I smile back, bending to unstrap Poppy from her stroller.

"Hiya! I didn't know you had a baby."

The boy squeezes past me, and I nudge the stroller out of his way.

"Yes." I straighten, now holding Poppy, who eyes everyone in the room suspiciously. "This is Poppy."

"What a sweet name." The woman twinkles at Poppy. "I'm Vivian. I own the café."

She reaches out a hand, and I take it. Vivian is pretty, with thick black hair that sports a few threads of silver. Her warm complexion and gray-green, almond-shaped eyes give her a feline quality. Her huge smile draws me in like a hug.

"Hi, Vivian, I'm Cordy Brown. We just moved here. Do you know if anyone ordered some honeybees recently?"

Vivian frowns. "No, I don't think so. Why?"

I explain the whole bee debacle to a stunned Vivian. I can see the elderly couple tune in. They both keep shooting me side looks of interest.

"And he just left them with you?" Vivian asks, aghast. "Prat," she adds under her breath.

I nod. "Yep. He said he wouldn't transport the bees back to wherever they came from."

"What are you going to do with them?"

"I have absolutely no idea," I admit. "I've never taken care of bees before. I don't even know if I have to feed or water them."

"Barney might be able to help you."

I turn to the old man who spoke up. "Who's Barney?"

"Jack Nelson's father," Vivian supplies. "He used to tend bees back in the eighties."

The old woman jumps in. "I thought he had bees in the seventies."

"Was it? I'm not sure. Either way, it was long before my time here." Vivian shrugs.

"He's in his eighties now himself," the man says. "But he's sure to have some tips and literature to share with you."

"Where does Barney live?" I ask. "Could he have ordered some bees?"

The old man chortles. "Oh, no. Barney can't see anymore, can he? Gone blind about three years ago. He's not likely to have any more bees. But, as I said, he's still as sharp as a tack and would have some advice."

"He lives up past the employment office," Vivian says. "Past that big bend in the road. He has a sweet little cottage off to the right."

"Do you think he would mind if we dropped in?" I ask.

"Aw no, love. Barney would love the company." The old man smiles at me.

Vivian hurries back behind the counter. "Here, I'll make you a cup of coffee to go. It's a bit of a walk, and you'll need the energy."

"Oh, I—"

"On the house," Vivian says easily as she caps the to-go cup. "You're having a stressful morning."

"Well, thank you, Vivian." I take the cup from her and smile. "Thanks a lot, really."

"Of course." Vivian helps me buckle Poppy back into her stroller. "And here, can Poppy have a sugar cookie?"

When I nod, Vivian hands a grinning Poppy the treat. With an elegant flick of her wrist she shoos us out. "Now then, go learn about bees."

The walk up to Barney Nelson's home *is* long. I have to take two breaks along the way, each time pausing in the shade of trees growing near the road. Poppy doesn't seem to mind the walk and plays with her toy pony. She polished off her cookie in about five seconds and only whined minimally for a second one. Even the coffee Vivian gave me is good. It doesn't have as much cream and sugar as I normally put in, but it's one of the highlights of my morning. Not that there's a lot of competition.

I'm starting to feel a little cheerful. Optimistic, even. Maybe it's because I'm taking steps to solve a problem. I can't do much about the job situation except wait and apply for jobs and wait some more. But I can try to figure out how to raise bees. Or tend bees, or whatever the proper terminology is.

Finally, we reach the bend in the road Vivian mentioned. Within a few minutes, a small cottage comes into view on the right, and I speed up in excitement.

Okay. I'm probably hoping for too much in meeting Barney Nelson. I'm not even sure what I hope he'll be able to do for me. A tiny part of me takes in his overgrown garden and wonders if he needs a gardener. Then again, it's not as if a blind man in his eighties will hire me to clean a garden he can't see.

Giving Poppy's stroller a little extra push, I hurry up the short driveway and to the small paved path that leads to the front door. I set the stroller on the path and unbuckle Poppy. She flails excitedly, ready to be free of her constraints. Hoisting her onto my hip, I make my way to the green front door.

Using the old-fashioned brass knocker, I wait for an answer. I can't even hear sounds of someone moving around inside. I don't want to be a creep and look into the windows, so I stand nervously in front of the door, holding a squirming baby.

Poppy is determined to get down and waddle through the grass, but I hold tightly to her. She lets out a huge whine just as the door opens.

"Hello?"

Barney Nelson is thin and slightly stooped, but I can tell that in his younger years he was a large and powerfully built man. His square jaw holds the hint of those days. Huge glasses perch on his nose, which I find odd, given he's supposed to be blind. His white hair is still thick and is cut short. Overall, he looks fit for a man in his eighties.

"Hi, Mr. Nelson. I'm Cordy Brown, and this is my daughter, Poppy." Poppy, thankfully, has stopped squirming and is now staring at Barney Nelson.

"Oh, call me Barney," Barney says cheerily. He's looking right at my face, and seeing my confused expression, he raises an eyebrow.

"I'm sorry for staring. It's just that someone told me you're blind." I blush furiously. Great, I'll open with talking about this poor man's blindness. Or lack thereof. *Great job, Cordy.*

Barney snorts. "You must have been talking to one of those old heads in the village, eh? They all like to say I'm far worse off than I really am. Not sure why, as none of them ever offer to help a supposedly old blind man with one leg."

I look down at what appears to be his two solid legs. Barney laughs again. "I have both my legs and most of my vision. Don't listen to anyone over the age of forty, all right?" He turns and beckons us in. "Come in, come in! I'll make us some proper tea."

I follow Barney inside and look around the small cottage. It's simple, only a few pieces of furniture here and there. A large grandfather clock dominates the room. Even though it's set against the wall, it protrudes into the room, a deep clicking reminding everyone of its presence.

A small kitchen attaches to the living room, and it appears to be just as sparse as this room. The walls are free of pictures. A kettle sits on the stove, and Barney busies himself in his cabinets. I look at the grandfather clock again and then around the rest of the room. It seems lonely with no pictures or art on the walls.

"Want some sugar in your tea?" Barney is already carrying two cups of tea from the kitchen. He offers me the pale blue one with a saucer.

"Oh, yes, please." I take the cup and glance between the tartan armchair by the empty fireplace and the maroon armchair by the window.

"Take whichever seat you want, love." Barney holds out a jar full of sugar cubes.

"Ah, could you—?" I hold out my cup, my other hand still holding onto Poppy, who is mercifully not squirming right now. "Two, please."

Barney drops two sugar cubes into my cup. "So, Carrie—"

"Cordy."

"Excuse me." He winks at me. "My memory isn't what it used to be. Ms. Cordy. What can I do for you?"

After settling down in the maroon armchair and handing Poppy a biscuit and two plush toys from her diaper bag, I tell him about the bees. The more I talk, the more I want to cry. I mean, really? Bees?

"But, anyway. Vivian at the café and the elderly couple seemed to think you might have some books on bees or something . . ." I trail off awkwardly and sip my tea. It's lavender, I realize with pleasure. I take another drink of the sweet, smoky liquid and wait for Barney to impart some wisdom.

Barney swirls his tea in his little chipped mug, frowning thoughtfully. "Do you think the past owners might have purchased the bees?"

I sit up in the surprisingly comfy armchair. "Do you think so? I could call the real estate agent and ask."

Barney points. "I have a phone in the kitchen, if you'd like to use it."

Digging my cell phone out of my pocket, I check to see if I have a signal. When my phone shows I don't, I hurry to the kitchen.

"Thank you," I call to Barney as I dial the number for the agency I have saved in my contacts. Not that I'll ever use them again after this disastrous buy.

Poppy gets up on her chubby legs and toddles after me, whimpering that I've left her. Reaching out, I pick her up and cuddle her against my chest as Barney's phone rings. After three rings, a woman's voice comes on the line.

"Hello?"

"Hi, I need to speak to the agent who sold me the house in Arbury."

The woman sighs. "Ms. Brown?"

I quell the urge to laugh at her tone. The agency received a semi-hysterical call when I realized I hadn't gotten the address wrong and was indeed at the house I had purchased. After a series of phone calls, each with me furiously explaining I had moved all the way from London with my infant daughter to be hoodwinked into a house with a Swiss-cheese roof, the lovely people at the agency had finally caved.

At first, they'd told me they weren't liable if I hadn't taken the time to come and see the house in person, but after getting a hold of the supervisor of the agent who'd sold me the house, I was able to convince them it wasn't fair given the clearly outdated video the agent had sent me. In return for my watery roof and broken windows, they refunded me part of the agent's commission and placed the agent under strict surveillance to prevent him from selling houses under false pretenses again.

"Yes," I tell the receptionist now. "This is Ms. Brown, but I only want to find out if the previous owners left a forwarding address or phone number. I just received a delivery I didn't order, and I wanted to see if it was theirs."

"I'm sorry, Ms. Brown, but I can't give you that information."

I start to protest, but the droll voice on the line continues. "Even if I could, it wouldn't matter. The previous owners moved out nearly six months ago. I highly doubt a package that late would be for them."

"Oh." Six months is a very long time.

"Is that all, Ms. Brown?"

"I . . . I guess so."

"Then, good day."

The line goes dead, and the feeble hope that the bees will be leaving me dies too.

"No luck?" Barney shakes his head sympathetically as I come back to sit down.

Poppy immediately squirms out of my arms and onto the floor to play with her toys. I watch her, feeling frustrated. What am I supposed to do with a bunch of bees?

"Well." Barney has gotten up from his seat and moves around to a small bookshelf tucked next to the grandfather clock. "Looks like you've got some bees to tend to now, don't you?"

I blink at him. "I can't raise bees, Barney."

After studying the shelf for a few moments, Barney pulls four books from the shelf and walks back to me. Placing the books in my hands, he grins at me. "Sure you can. You'll love it!"

Chapter Three
Cordy

Barney's confidence still hasn't soaked in by the time I make it back home. He gave me a brief explanation of honeybees and showed me some key parts of the books he thought I'd need most. Then he sent me on my way and told me he would call Jack to come over and help move the bees into the backyard.

I protested moving the bees at first, citing the fact that they were liable to sting anyone who tried to move them.

Barney squinted at me in surprise. "Are they up and flying about? They can be cheeky if they're flying."

"I . . . I don't know. Do bees sleep during the day?" I couldn't remember anything about bees being nocturnal.

"No, but when bees are being transported, whoever sends them out smokes them." Seeing my confused expression, he continued with a grin. "Beekeepers puff a bit of smoke into hives to disorient the bees. The smoke usually lasts about half an hour though, so I thought they'd be up and about by now."

"Does that mean the bees came from somewhere close? Maybe I could find out who sent them."

Barney raised an eyebrow at me. "Or you could become a beekeeper, Cordy."

So here I am, trudging back home with a sleepy baby, semi-ready to be a beekeeper.

An old green truck is sitting in my driveway, and I suspect it's Jack coming to help move the bees into the backyard. As I reach the bumper of the truck, I see him standing over the hives, holding something silver in his hands. It appears to be a cross between a teapot and an old coffee can.

"Good afternoon, Ms. Brown," Jack says cheerfully. His Santa-ish appearance is magnified by the red plaid shirt he's wearing.

"Hi, Jack." I stop a good distance from the beehives and angle Poppy's stroller away from any possible irate bugs. "What are you doing?"

"Smoking them before I move them." He waves the canister in his hand. I notice the spout at the top has a thin stream of smoke coming out.

"Oh, okay."

"Mama." Poppy reaches for me, and I unbuckle her. Holding her on my hip, we both watch Jack. He blows smoke into a small slit of an opening at the bottom of the hives. Stretching onto my tiptoes, I try to see exactly what he's doing.

"See here, lass?" Jack looks up and waves me over. Hesitantly, I edge around his truck into my front yard. The hives are silent.

I notice now the hives, which I'd originally thought resembled stacked shelves, are just boxes stacked one on another. There are six boxes per hive, and they sit on a small wooden platform that juts out a couple of inches at the bottom, creating a tiny porch for the bees. All four hives are painted the same pale blue, which is quite pretty.

One fat little bee wobbles around on the platform of the hive closest to us. It appears to be drunk.

Pointing at the bee, I say, "Is that what happens to all the bees when you smoke them?"

Jack nods. "They think their hive might be catching fire, actually, so they try to gather as much honey as possible, eating it as they go. The disorienting effect of the smoke and their heavy bellies eventually leads them to lie down."

"They think their hive is on fire?" I can't help but feel alarmed. "It seems cruel to trick them into thinking they're about to die."

With a grunt, Jack lifts one of the hives. "Well, would you rather carry a hive with all the bees awake and alert?"

He sets the hive onto a box cart and reaches for the next one. I don't have an answer, so I watch him silently as he moves two hives at a time. Following him into the backyard, I look around for a good place to set the hives.

"What about over here?" I point to where an oak tree semi-shades a corner of the yard. The tree is actually on the other side of the fence, but its branches are so large, they give a nice shade to my yard.

With some effort, given my horribly overgrown grass, Jack pushes the box cart over to the shade. Instead of putting the hives down, he waves at me to wait and heads to his truck. Within a few minutes, he's back, holding a cinder block in each hand. Setting the blocks parallel to each other, he gently lifts one of the hives and places it on the blocks.

"The blocks will keep the hives dry when it rains," he explains.

"Thanks, Jack. For all your help."

He shoots me a wink. "Anything to help the new beekeeper, lass. My dad seemed keen on you too, so that of course helps."

"I'm not sure I'd call myself a beekeeper," I hedge.

Jack seems not to have heard me. He's got a faraway look in his eyes and chews wistfully on the corner of his mustache.

"Ay, Dad did make some good honey back in the day. And Ma's honey cakes had all the village children rounded up at her front door every Saturday morning."

There's a moment of silence as Jack reminisces, and I try to keep Poppy from pulling herself up onto a beehive. A sleepy-looking bee totters out of the hive to sit on its little porch thing. I scoop up a whining Poppy and back away.

Okay, even though I'm now Arbury's new beekeeper, the little bugs kind of terrify me. Haven't I read somewhere that if one stings you, all the others follow suit? Something about a hormone attracting and alerting the other bees to sting.

I mean, how is that not terrifying?

Snapping to, Jack swipes his ball cap from his head and nods at me. "I'll grab the last two hives and be on my way."

Feeling a little useless, I watch Jack maneuver the last two hives into the backyard. He gets more cinder blocks from his truck as well, and soon I'm staring at my brand new hives, cozied up in my backyard. Jack gives me stern instructions not to let Poppy unattended around the hives—as if I'd ever—and wishes me luck.

"Thanks again, Jack," I call as he retreats to his truck. He shoots me one last wave before driving away.

Poppy gives an almighty wriggle and with a sigh, I hurry her to the kitchen door and inside. Setting her on the much safer kitchen floor, I close the door and stare out at the hives. They look innocent enough, except I know full-well all of them are chock-full of insects that could probably kill me.

Maybe that's a little dramatic.

"What am I supposed to do now, Pops?" I mumble as I start getting her lunch ready. My only answer is the clanking of a wooden spoon on a pot as Poppy plays a feisty melody. That's pretty much what my brain sounds like right now anyway.

Chapter Four
Ronan

"You can't be serious."

I stare at the mess my brother calls a bathroom. Toothpaste is caked to the inside of the sink, spittle covers the mirror, discarded towels (and . . . is that a pair of boxers?) litter the floor, and there appears to be some sort of mold growing in the tub.

"Corwynn," I shout. No answer. I try again. "Corwynn!"

"What?" The muffled reply comes from his bedroom down the hall.

"How do you live like this? Is this why you left? So you could make a mess without listening to Mam telling you to clean it up?"

A muffled reply that sounds a lot like 'shut up' reaches me.

"Mam would have a heart attack," I grumble as I kick a sock. In response to my kick, something moves in the corner of the room.

"You've got rodents living in this house." I shout at him again, watching the corner for more signs of life.

"That's Cheddar," Corwynn's voice booms back. "Leave 'im be."

He's named the rats that live in this sty he calls a home. Mam wouldn't just have a heart attack if she saw this, she'd keel over, then rise from the dead to murder Corwynn.

And is this the thanks I get? Rats?

I can only be thankful that it's the summer holiday. If I had to put in a request for a sabbatical, that would have started a whole new set of problems. The University of Dublin, where I teach Agricultural History of Ireland, may like me, but I'm not sure they'd let me traipse off to find my runaway brother. Yet, here I find him holed up with *rats* in a town that isn't even on a map. The only reason I came after Corwynn was because Mam begged me to, and I can't say no to her. She can't come after him herself since Da's taken sick, but I, the older and more responsible brother, can.

I try to infuse calm into my voice as I walk to his room and peer into the equally messy space. "You can't take off like that, mate. You're still underage, and you've got exams to finish."

I arrived at Corwynn's tiny flat last night, but it was so late, I couldn't get a word in before he told me he had to sleep. Apparently, he has work in the morning. Who in their right mind would hire a seventeen-year-old is beyond me.

Well, that's hardly fair. He is of hiring age, and he's a massive lad. He did say something about working on a farm last night, which makes sense. Mam and Da have had a sheep farm since I was old enough to walk. Neither of us is inexperienced when it comes to lifting heavy things and chasing animals.

But even if Corwynn was the most skilled farmer the world's ever seen, he's still got exams, and he can't abandon all of his responsibilities and run away from his home.

I kick the lump on the floor that is my brother. "Do you hear me?"

I think he's sleeping on a mattress, but it's hard to tell with the amount of clothes on the floor.

Corwynn's head rises from the blankets. "I'm not taking the exams."

"You are being ridiculous—"

He glares at me. "Look, Ronan, the only reason you care is because Mam told you to care. But you don't have to. You can go back to having your head up your—"

It's my turn to interrupt him. "I do care."

With a snort, he rolls over, facing the wall away from me. "Well, if you care so much, you'd leave me to sleep so I can do a good job at work."

I stare at the back of my little brother's head. How did I let Mam talk me into this?

I have not admitted defeat. I've just decided to pick and choose my battles, and this isn't one I care to fight. I'm not going to drag Corwynn back home even though I want to, because he'll take off again. And next time I won't find him.

Instead, I'm in his filthy kitchen. Which is better than his bathroom, but not by much. I find a mug that looks clean, and Corwynn's coffee maker spews out something that resembles coffee. It fills the stale air with a burnt smell. *When was the last time he cleaned his coffee maker?*

I take one sip and immediately spit the stuff out. For some reason, it's tangy and has a rubbery aftertaste. How does one even achieve that? I wouldn't give this to someone I hate. No one deserves that.

The truth is, coffee needs to be made a specific way. You can't just throw some subpar grounds into a coffee machine and call it good. Coffee is meant to be savored, and nothing made from a tin will do.

There's a slim possibility this town has a coffee shop, but I'm tempted to go find out. A loud bang draws my attention, and Corwynn tumbles into the kitchen. He's disheveled, but he's dressed. Then I see what he's holding.

"Corwynn. What is that?" I try to sound as if I'm asking a reasonable question.

Looking unruffled, Corwynn nods down at the animal. "It's a goat, ain't it?"

"Why do you have a goat? Where did it come from?"

"Had it, didn't I?"

"But where?" I stare at him.

"Next to my bed. Its mam didn't want it and Jack couldn't keep it, so I took it home. I couldn't let it die."

That's my little brother. He's pigheaded and messy, but he loves animals and would do anything to keep them safe. Including taking them home to his tiny flat, where I'm sure he's not allowed to have animals.

"Who is Jack?" I ask.

"My boss. He's a farmer out on the edge of town."

"Corwynn," I start gently. "You can't keep a goat. Not here. It needs grass, and I'm sure you're breaking your lease by having it." I see Corwynn's chin jut out in defiance. Hurriedly, I add, "I can take it. I'll find it a home, okay?"

Surprise lifts his eyebrows. "You'll help?"

"Yeah." I hold out my arms. "Here, give it to me. I've got to find a decent cup of coffee anyway. This stuff is poison."

Rolling his eyes, Corwynn hands the little animal over to me. It snuffles at my hand and makes a bleating noise. It has the longest ears I've ever seen, but it is cute. Soft, white fur covers its body, and brown markings around its eyes and nose gives it the appearance of smiling. I ruffle the long ears, the tips of which are also brown.

"All right then." I nod. "I'm off to find this orphan a home."

Corwynn ignores this statement and walks back toward his room.

The goat doesn't seem to mind a different person carrying it, and chews on the cuff of my jacket. With my new friend, I walk down the road toward the center of the village. The small grocery store I saw when I first drove in might have a few people who could at least point me in the direction of someone needing a goat.

The goat nudges me with its head and shoots me a look that is clearly telling me off for being so short with Corwynn. Of course it would take his side.

"Don't give me that look," I grumble. "I'm trying to keep him from ruining his life."

The goat doesn't seem impressed by my explanation. Animals were never my strong suit anyway. Growing up on a farm, I found myself more often reading than actually playing with the animals. I was twelve when Corwynn came along, and by the time he wanted to play, I had discovered the cute neighbor girl.

I'll admit, I wouldn't win any awards for "best brother." The age gap didn't help, and Corwynn spent more time with the sheep than he did with me. Then I was in college and never saw him. I can see why Corwynn feels like I never cared much for him, but I do. Of course I do. Unfortunately, I'm not good at showing it.

Not that the goat needs to hear all of that. It would probably still side with him anyway.

Before the goat can give me another reproving look, I've made it to the grocer's. It seems pretty bare, but I do spot an elderly man checking out.

"Excuse me." I pause in front of him and the tired-looking clerk. "Do either of you know someone who'd like a goat?"

The goat perks up and bleats cheerfully from my arms. The clerk looks alarmed. "Sir, we can't have no goats in here."

"I'm just trying to find it a home."

The clerk shakes his head, his messy red hair flying. "No, sir. Please remove the goat."

Oh, for Pete's sake. "The goat won't hurt anything. It's a baby," I snap at the quivering clerk.

The elderly man speaks up. "Take her down to the coffee shop. Vivian knows everybody in town. She'd be likely to know who needs a wee little goat." He chuffs the goat under the chin.

I smile at him, because at least he isn't cowering from a five-pound animal. "Thank you. I can't wait to have some good coffee anyway."

Leaving the relieved clerk behind, I exit the grocer's and head in the direction the elderly man pointed. It's only a minute's walk before I climb the steps to the Bluebell Café. It's cozy, although it smells strongly of lemons. I don't normally associate lemons with a coffee shop, but I'm more interested in meeting Vivian and finding my tagalong a home.

A woman behind the small counter smiles at me. "Welcome."

"Hi, are you Vivian?"

When she nods, I hold up the goat. "I need to find this little goat a home."

She grins. "I know just the place."

This can't be right. The house Vivian sent me to looks like it should be condemned. Some of the windows are covered in what looks like tarp, which I assume means the glass is broken. The roof needs to be rethatched, and overgrown grass swallows the yard.

But I double-check the number on the mailbox with the one Vivian wrote on a slip of paper, and it is the same.

"Well then, are you ready for your new home?" I ask the goat.

It turns out Vivian is some sort of goat expert—at least, she's taken care of one before—and she's sent me with three bottles of milk and the information that the goat is a girl. She also mentioned the person at this address would probably have a bottle to use for feeding the goat. Based on the shape of the house, I'm not sure why she would assume whoever lives here has anything.

Tone it down, Ronan. I step over the crooked little gate. Mam always said I was a bit sour in the mornings. I blame today's sourness on the lack of proper coffee. I'd been so swept up in the excitement of finding this goat whisperer that I didn't even buy a cup of coffee at the Bluebell Café.

And while I shouldn't judge the owner of the house, I do want to know who could live here and be happy. Broken, drafty windows can hardly be comfortable.

I barely finish knocking on the surprisingly sturdy-looking front door when it swings open. For a moment, I stand frozen, my hand still poised to knock.

Now, this makes even less sense. The woman standing in front of me is beautiful. She appears to be a little younger than myself and has hair I can only describe as flowing. It ripples down her shoulders and hits at her waist. It's also the color of wheat, something I've always found appealing.

Her pale hair frames intensely blue eyes, a slim nose, and a full mouth. She looks like a runaway princess holed up in a witch's cottage.

"Good morning?" She has an American accent, but I note it's not the normal flat-toned, annoying accent. It's somehow soft and sweet, much more like a vintage Scarlett O'Hara.

Get it together, Ronan. I mentally shake myself. I don't know this woman at all, and here I am drooling after her as if she's a siren rescuing me from drowning. Pathetic.

"Good morning, ma'am." I noticed her mouth twitch into a half-smile. "I was told you may want this goat."

Smooth, Ronan.

She blinks at me. "Goat?"

I hold up the creature, who gives a little sound of surprise and stares at the woman. I can't blame the goat. The woman is quite stunning.

"I don't know anything about goats. I'm sorry, I'm not sure who told you I wanted a goat—"

"Please, ma'am. It's an orphan, and Vivian sent along some milk for it. She said she'll supply you with milk as long as you need."

"Vivian? Vivian sent you here?"

I nod. "She said something about you being good with small things and that you'd already have a bottle to use for feeding."

The woman stares at me. After a moment of chewing on her bottom lip, she nods. "Okay, I guess I can try to raise it. Especially if Vivian promises to get me milk."

"Grand, thank you." I try to hand the goat over, but she turns away from me into the house of horrors.

"Come on in; I'll get her set up in the kitchen. Oh"— she glances back at me—"is it a girl or a boy?"

"A girl." I follow her inside. Just as I suspected, there are buckets on the floor under where I guess the roof is leaking. Besides the holes in the roof and windows, I'm surprised to find a cozy, if sparse, home.

"I'm sorry, I don't think I got your name?" the woman calls from her kitchen.

"Ronan. Ronan Thomson."

"Hi, Ronan, nice to meet you." She grins at me as I enter the kitchen. It appears to be the most lived-in of the rooms. "I'm Cordy Brown."

"Cordy, nice to meet you too." I spot a stuffed bunny on the kitchen table. Next to it lies a board book and a handful of wooden blocks.

Ah. Of course a woman like her wouldn't be single. I try to push all images of her mouth out of my head. I can't go kissing a married woman in my mind. Although . . . I glance at her hand. She isn't wearing a ring. Maybe she's the kind who doesn't like wedding rings. Or she isn't married to the father of the baby who obviously lives here. Or she's a single mother. Or she's just babysitting.

The possibilities seem endless. All I want to know is if she's single. There has to be a way of finding out if she is or not.

"Cute bunny." I point to the stuffed toy on the table.

Glancing up from where she's carefully pouring some of the milk into a baby bottle, Cordy smiles. "Yeah, that's one of my daughter's favorites. Her absolute favorite is her pony. She's napping right now with it."

"How old is your daughter?" I'm genuinely curious. Corwynn has always been good with animals, but I've always been good with kids.

"Ten months! I feel like her birthday is coming up so quickly."

I watch Cordy's face brighten as she talks about her daughter's upcoming birthday. Something hopeful stirs in my heart. I try to push it back. We still haven't established her relationship status.

"Here." Cordy hands me the bottle. "Try this."

I offer the bottle to the goat, who blinks at me.

"Take a little milk from the nipple and wipe it on her nose," Cordy instructs. "I had to help raise an orphaned kitten once when I was nine," she adds when I raise an eyebrow at her.

I do as I'm told. The goat licks at her nose, then tentatively sniffs the bottle. I try touching the bottle to her nose again, and this time she licks at the milk. Then, as if discovering manna, the goat latches onto the milk and with little jerky head movements, begins to suckle.

"Yes!" Cordy claps her hands in excitement.

I fight the urge to beam at her. *Tone it down, Ronan.*

A yell interrupts our glee, and it takes me a second to realize the yell is coming from another room. It must be Cordy's daughter waking up from her nap.

"Hold on," Cordy calls as she hurries from the kitchen. She's back in a moment, holding a grinning baby. She's the cutest child I've ever seen.

"Poppy, this is Ronan. Ronan, this is my daughter, Poppy."

Poppy shrieks, waving at the goat, who lets go of the bottle to stare at the newcomer.

"You see the goat?" Cordy points to the goat, who goes back to eating.

Poppy wiggles furiously in her mam's arms, and Cordy sets her down. The little girl toddles to me and grips my pants to stare up at the goat. Gently squatting down, I show Poppy the goat.

"She looks just like you," I say to Cordy. She looks pleased, but I'm not saying it to flatter her. Poppy has the same large blue eyes and fine blonde hair as her mother. Her cheeks have dimples, which are different from Cordy's, and they give her a picture-perfect quality.

"This goat is going to live with you," I tell Poppy. She stares wide-eyed at the animal.

The goat finishes her breakfast and squirms to be let down. I glance at Cordy, who nods, so I place the animal down. Poppy squeals as the goat bounces on the tile floor.

"I better be going," I say, straightening up.

"I can walk you out." Cordy gestures to the buckets set strategically around the living room floor. "I don't want you to trip."

I see my opportunity and seize it. "If your husband needs help fixing some of these leaks, I can help him."

"Oh." Her cheeks go pink. "I don't have a husband. I mean, I don't . . . I'm single."

I fight to keep a grin from breaking out. "Ah, well, I can come back after lunch and fix some of these holes that have made their way into your roof."

"Really?" Her eyes light up, but then she quickly shakes her head. "I can't ask you to do that, not on your day off."

"I'm actually on summer holiday. I teach history at the University of Dublin, and I'm on a mission to get my younger brother. He's seventeen and ran away last week. I'm here to bring him back—" I cut myself off. She doesn't want to hear all of my family drama. "Anyway, it'll take a few days to convince him to come home and take his exams. In the meantime, I can fix your roof."

"I can't pay you." Cordy chews on her perfect lips. "I . . . well, I just lost my job, and we moved here last week. I didn't know what kind of condition the house would be in. The realtor sent me a video, and I thought it was recent. I haven't gotten a new job yet either."

"You moved in a week ago?"

"Yeah, why?"

I shrug. "From the way Vivian spoke of you, I thought you were some village goat whisperer."

She flushes again. "I mean, I'm not a goat killer or anything. I'm not going to hurt her."

"I didn't say you were!"

"If you don't want to leave her here—"

"I didn't say that either." I shake my head quickly. "Look, I'll be back in a couple of hours to fix the roof. I don't require payment. No woman and absolutely no child should live like this. You'll both catch pneumonia."

A small smile finally curves her lips. "Okay, then. Thank you, Ronan."

I wink at her. "My pleasure."

Chapter Five
Cordy

We've named the goat Go-go because it's easy for Poppy to say. She adores Go-go, and it appears Go-go adores my daughter just as much. They've been running around the house like crazies ever since Ronan left.

I know what you're thinking. I know nothing about goats. But goats are like dogs, right? Feed them, water them, let them exercise. Do goats like to play fetch?

Anyway, it'll be fine. Go-go is pretty cute. Although I have already had to shoo her down from the kitchen table twice. I'm not even sure how she got up there to begin with. Also, she's not exactly potty trained, but I'll have to figure that out later. Maybe Barney knows how to potty train goats.

I don't have time to go to Barney's and ask him though, because now I have to get ready for Ronan to come back.

Ronan.

Has a more attractive man ever existed?

He's nothing like Poppy's dad, which is probably a good thing. Poppy's dad is also blond like me and is pretty average in most regards. Not that there's anything wrong with average. I do think I loved him before. I'm just saying he's average.

Ronan, on the other hand, is very tall and dark. He has a beard. I've never been attracted to a man with a beard before. That in itself is pretty new for me. It's a very well-kept beard, and it's not as dark as his neatly trimmed hair. It even has little streaks of red in it, which is pretty fascinating.

Do you hear me? Beards are now fascinating. The first cute guy to cross my path, and I'm fixated on his facial hair. What is wrong with me?

Even if I have a weird thing for his slightly red beard, I'm guessing Ronan isn't interested in me. I didn't see a ring, but attractive men like him are usually attached.

So instead of picturing myself on a date with him, I decide to use my energy to clean my house as much as I can. It may have leaks and holes, but the floors are swept and the toys and clothes that are normally discarded on the floor are now picked up.

I used to be very neat. Poppy has changed that. I'm also going to hazard a guess that having an indoor goat won't help matters either.

I contain Go-go and Poppy in the kitchen, where Poppy is sharing her animal crackers with her new friend. Go-go seems to like them more than Poppy, and is cheerfully snuffling them out of my daughter's hands.

At least they're happy.

Now, I know animal crackers aren't a proper lunch, but I also don't have a lot of options right now. Also, they're not strictly unhealthy, so I'm chalking this up to a good snack while I try to come up with something other than oatmeal for lunch.

Most of my cupboards are bare, which puts a small dent into my I-saw-a-cute-guy high. When is the employment office going to call? Is there seriously no one hiring? I can't keep eking out my savings and surviving on oatmeal and animal crackers.

I decide to make oatmeal again (I doubt Poppy will remember she had it for breakfast . . . right?) when there's a knock at the door for the second time today.

"Stay put, you two." I shake a finger at Poppy, who is too busy laughing over Go-go to notice.

Pulling open my door, I find Ronan standing there. Instantly, I'm keenly aware of his broad shoulders blocking out the weak afternoon light. And then I'm aware I need to stop staring.

"Oh, I thought you weren't going to be back for another hour or so." I gabble to cover my drooling. Shoulders have always been a weak spot of mine.

He holds up a bag. "I thought I'd share my lunch with you ladies, if that's all right. I don't know anyone in town besides my brother, and he's not exactly excited by my presence. Would you mind?"

I'm smart enough to know he probably caught on to my not having very much money, and wants to make sure Poppy and I get something to eat today. I also know this is a kind gesture, and my daughter will appreciate eating something other than oatmeal.

"We'd love to." I step back to let him in. "Poppy might even share some of her animal crackers with you if Go-go hasn't eaten them all."

"Go-go?"

"The goat."

"Ah." He laughs. "That's a fun name."

I lead him to the kitchen. "It helps that Poppy can say it."

"Mama!" Poppy cheers as Ronan and I enter the kitchen. I love that little girl so much.

Ronan sets his bag on the countertop. Go-go takes this as an opportunity to spring onto the table.

"No, Go-go!" I swat at the goat, who jumps nimbly to the floor again.

Ronan laughs—a deep, soul-rumbling sound. Immediately, I promise to make him laugh again, just to hear that infectious sound.

"Are you ladies hungry?" Ronan is still chuckling at Go-go, who is now circling him like a dog looking for treats.

From the bag, he pulls out a box of donuts, three boxes of macaroni and cheese, a frozen pizza, and all the ingredients for sandwiches. I stare as each item is placed on the worn kitchen table.

"That's a lot of food," I venture.

"I wasn't sure what you all like to eat. Whatever we don't eat, we can save for dinner." He flushes. "I don't mean to invite myself to dinner, but I'm not sure how long it'll take to fix the leaks."

"You're absolutely invited to dinner," I say quickly. "You're doing us a huge favor."

Pizza seems to be the clear winner, and as the oven preheats, I store all the other food away for later. Ronan begins looking at the largest leak in the living room. He's even got a ladder with him. I want to ask if he normally travels with a ladder, but I have a sneaking suspicion that he bought it especially for this task.

I've never seen pizza eaten so quickly. I catch Poppy semi-discreetly offering her pepperoni to Go-go, who has clearly recognized Poppy as her food source.

"So, did you say you taught at the University of Dublin?" I wipe pizza sauce from the corner of my mouth and smile at Ronan.

"Yes, I've been teaching there for nearly six years." Ronan's face lights up. "I grew up near Killarney on a sheep farm. When I moved three hours north to work in Dublin, Mam was distraught. Da didn't mind much. He always knew I was more into reading books than raising sheep. Plus, they thought my brother would take over the farm."

"But he doesn't want it?"

"I'm not sure what he wants." Ronan shakes his head remorsefully. "Ay, anyway. I like Dublin, but being here has made me miss being in a small town. I miss the quiet."

"Well, there's plenty of that here." I snort. "This has to be the sleepiest town I've ever been in."

"Don't you like it?"

I take a moment to think about his question. "I liked that London has lots to offer. They have a million mommy-and-me type classes, and there are playgrounds everywhere. It was nice that most things were within walking distance. But public transport was a nightmare. I was always terrified that someone would try to grab Poppy, and everything in the underground smelled like unwashed bodies." I wrinkle my nose at the memory.

"What do you like about Arbury?"

"You know, even though this village is the size of a postage stamp, I've met more people here than I ever met in London. And they're good people. Plus, it's nice that I'm not terrified of getting run over by a double-decker bus while walking with Poppy." I look down at my squirming daughter. She's only eaten the cheese off of her pizza.

"Safety and good people sounds like a right fine place to me," Ronan says.

"Don't forget that it doesn't smell like B.O." I laugh.

"If you ever meet my brother, you might change your mind." Ronan winks and stands to clear the dishes. I get up to help. I have to admit, living here is starting to look better than London. Even with the leaky roof.

As soon as the dishes are picked up and placed in the sink to soak—all dishes need to soak for a minimum of four hours in my house—Ronan heads back to whatever he's doing to the leaks. I take the time to study up on beekeeping while Poppy and Go-go watch Curious George on my phone.

Barney's books have proven to be incredibly helpful. One of the books even has diagrams of bee flight patterns. I'm not sure if I really need to know that, but it's cool.

It turns out you do need to feed bees when there aren't many flowers. All I need to do is mix up a sugar-water syrup. Which sounds easy enough. I'm still not entirely sure how to feed it to the bees. Do I set out a teeny tiny bowl?

An image of a teeny tiny patio set for bees pops into my head, and I chuckle over the idea of putting little patio furniture on their little hive porches. Luckily, it's still summer, and I don't have to figure out how to feed them yet.

I've also learned each hive has one queen, who seems to be the one who lays all the eggs. What a job. The queen is also the only reason bees will swarm. As in, if she decides to move, the rest of the bees go with her.

This fact makes me glance out the kitchen window at my hives, but they don't appear to have any mass exoduses happening.

Poppy takes that moment to bang her head on the table, and I settle onto the floor to hold her while she cries. Go-go scuttles around us, pausing to nibble on Poppy's socked foot. With a shriek of delight, Poppy forgets her banged head and begins a game of holding out her foot to Go-go, only to whip it away when the goat nibbles at her.

Putting her on the floor to play, I look up to see Ronan in the doorframe. "Oh, hi!"

"I heard crying and wanted to check on Poppy." He smiles. "It appears she's not grievously injured."

"No." I laugh. "She's fine. How's the leak coming?"

"I patched the first one. It took a mite longer than I expected. It'll probably take a few days to patch up the rest. Plus the windows. If I come back early in the morning, I could work on getting one of the windows and another leak patched."

A weird mix of pleasure and anxiety battles inside me. I do want him to come back . . . but if it takes that long to fix each hole, there's no way I'll ever be able to pay him back.

"Look, Ronan, I really appreciate you being willing to help, but I can't pay you. It wouldn't be right to expect you to work for free."

With a slow grin, he shakes his head. "Cordy, I haven't anything else to do. You'd be doing me a favor in letting me work on your house."

I narrow my eyes at him, but he continues to grin as if he genuinely means it.

"Okay. Fine. I can make you coffee in the morning then."

He winks. "I would accept coffee as a form of payment any day."

Chapter Six
Cordy

I need a plan. I can't keep hoping for a job and living off the ridiculous amounts of food Ronan keeps bringing by. Every day for the past week, he's shown up with arms laden with groceries and snacks. He might be Poppy and Go-go's hero. He's being very sweet about it, but I know he's worried Poppy and I will starve. I wouldn't let that happen, but I admit it's nice to have someone worry about us.

I almost scared Ronan off the first time I made him coffee. I made it the way I like, which turns out to be "an affront to good coffee everywhere." He tried to say it as if he was kidding, but I could see his pained face. Honestly, I don't mind, because *I* like the way I make coffee. But he did show up the next day with a French press, saying he was tired of terrible coffee. He offered to show me how to use it and I agreed, mostly because I wanted to be closer to him. I can't exactly follow him around my house as he patches it up, can I?

Because of Ronan's frequent trips to my house—i.e., every day—my house is now a good ten degrees warmer (turns out plugging holes is helpful), and my fridge is stocked. I've learned as much as I can about bees, and Barney even sent one of his old beekeeping suits to me by way of Jack. It fits surprisingly well and turned out to be Barney's late wife's. Apparently, he got it for her as a birthday present. She wore it once but was so scared of the bees, she packed the suit up and hid it from Barney. I can't say I blame her.

I tried out my new suit yesterday and attempted to look at the hives. I went during Poppy's naptime, because even if I had a toddler-sized suit, I would never take her near bees when I don't know what I'm doing.

And that's the truth, isn't it? I don't know what I'm doing. Not just with the bees, although they aren't as scary as I thought they'd be, but in life. The employment office *still* hasn't called. I thought they would have by now.

I realized last night I've been living in a weird little fairytale. One where I can stay home with Poppy and watch her play with a goat while a hunky man shows up each morning with food and a smile. If that doesn't sound like a movie script, I don't know what does. But it can't go on forever.

So today I'm sitting down and writing a list. One where I can figure out how to get a job. I might have to travel to another city to do it, but I am going to do it.

"What're you working on?" Ronan's deep voice makes me look up from my list. Poppy is taking a nap, and Go-go is sitting on one of my old sweaters in the corner of the kitchen, chewing cud. (It's gross. Vivian explained it to me. Don't ask.)

"I'm trying to get my life in order," I say seriously. "I can't sit around jobless forever."

Ronan reads over my shoulder. "'Marry a millionaire.' That sounds solid."

I groan and drop my pen on the table. "I don't know what to do. Why hasn't the employment office called? Are there no jobs in this town? Or the next one?"

"Have you asked around? Maybe someone local needs help with something."

"I already asked. That's the second thing I did after moving here. Jack was the only person hiring, but some jerk got the job before I did."

Ronan raises an eyebrow at me. "A jerk?"

"He was a jerk!" I exclaim. "He didn't smile once, but he was the better pick for the job. I can't throw hay bales into a barn loft. Which is why I plan to marry right," I add, trying to lighten the mood. "Do you have any millionaire cousins in need of a wife?"

Ronan's eyes darken, and he shakes his head slightly, not answering my question. I'm about to tell him I'm kidding when he straightens and looks directly at me.

"Why don't you make something? Can you knit?"

I stare at his hopeful expression for a moment before bursting into laughter. "I'm not a hundred years old. I can't knit."

He looks a little taken aback. "I can knit."

"You can knit?"

He plucks at the sweater he's wearing. "I knitted this last year."

I stare at him. "You knitted a whole sweater?"

He laughs. "No, my mam did. It was a Christmas present. I can't knit at all."

I smack his arm playfully. "Well, see? That's what I mean. Hardly anyone our age can knit."

"You should make a list of all the things you can do and would enjoy doing, and see if there's a service you can provide Arbury."

It's not much of a list. So far, I've come up with five things.

1. Baking
2. Cooking
3. Cleaning
4. Taking care of babies
5. Beekeeping. Maybe???

There's already a daycare which isn't hiring, and Vivian has a little café, which is sort of close to baking. I haven't figured out how to make money with beekeeping yet, and I did call Vivian to ask if there was anyone who cleaned houses in Arbury. She said that yes, Sydney Waterford's niece does. So. I'm back to square one.

Well, beekeeping is still a possibility, but I don't know what I'm doing. I've read the books, and I've even tried to look at the hives, but there's something still missing. Okay, I know what's missing—it's confidence. But I'm not sure how to build that up.

"This is hopeless." I set the list down with a groan.

From the living room, Ronan's ladder clanks. I listen to his footsteps as he comes into the kitchen. He leans over me to look at the list. "I think this looks quite good."

I pick up a pen to draw a line through the first four items. "I can't do any of these without pushing someone else's business to the side. Which isn't fair, given how small our community is. And this one"—I tap my pencil to *beekeeping*—"I don't know where to start."

"Hey, you don't need to rush." Ronan takes a seat across from me. "You're plenty smart and capable."

Reaching out, Ronan gently pats my hand. It's a little awkward, but endearing that he's trying to comfort me. I grin at him. "Oh yeah? You think I'm smart?"

"You've always got your nose in a book, don't you?" He gestures to the pile of bee books at the end of the table. "And I've seen you handle all sorts of conflicts with Poppy."

"Well, she's not even one, so it's mostly just distracting her with toys and giving kisses."

He shakes his head. "You're selling yourself short; that's conflict management right there."

I can't help but laugh. "Maybe you should write my resume for me."

Ronan winks as he gets up from the table. "If nothing else, you're a great mam. I'll let you get back to your list."

Watching him walk back into the living room, I wonder how much longer I'll get to see him before the house is patched up. Hopefully, he'll work slowly.

Most of the leaks have been fixed, and part of me thinks they could have all been fixed by now. It seems Ronan is stalling. Which is pretty nice. I like having him around. He hasn't been weird about Poppy, and he cracks jokes that make me laugh. I don't think I've smiled this much since I lost my job.

It's Saturday, and Ronan has taken today to try to get his brother to go home. Poppy, Go-go, and I head out for a walk up the street, something Go-go is pretty good at. I've already gotten her collar and leash trained, and she trots along next to Poppy's stroller like a strange little puppy. Most of the neighbors have come out to meet Go-go too. She's been a nice icebreaker.

We're nearing our house when I see Jack's pickup pulling in. I wave, and as he gets out of the truck, he waves back. Then I see he has someone in the passenger seat.

"Barney," I say, delighted. "How are you?"

I haven't been back to Barney's house since he gave me the books on bees. I've been meaning to. It's been a whirlwind couple of weeks, and I've had Ronan on my mind for most of them. I mentally kick myself. I've already forgotten one of the nicest people in town, and I resolve to do better from now on.

"Would you like to stay for dinner? I'm sorry I haven't been back to visit." I give him an apologetic wince.

Barney grins at me. "I'm doing well, lass, and there's no need to be sorry. Moving into this house has been quite the project, I'm sure. I came to check on how the bees are faring."

"They're fine, I think. They've been pretty active. I keep Poppy out of the backyard for the most part. I don't want her to get stung."

Barney waves toward the backyard. "Show me."

Within a few minutes, I've safely put Poppy and Go-go in the kitchen, slipped into my beekeeping uniform, and met Barney next to the hives. I can see my daughter and goat both watching me from the kitchen door. It's made of glass, which is usually covered in hand and nose prints, but is pretty helpful at keeping Poppy occupied.

Jack stands near the door, making faces at Poppy, who grins at him. Even with his help, I'm glad I put the baby gate up to keep her from wandering around the house.

Barney, very thoughtfully, has brought along some equipment for me. He hands me a box full of tools as I come out of the house in my suit.

"This is a hive tool." He holds up a flat metal object that looks like a mini crowbar. "You use it to pry open the hive. Bees tend to seal their hives shut."

"To keep us out?"

He shrugs. "To keep out drafts and badgers too."

"That makes it seem like we're stealing," I say nervously.

"Lass, the bees make an overabundance of honey. A good beekeeper does not take all the honey, as a badger would. Instead, we leave some for them as well. It's more like sharing than stealing." Barney smiles kindly. "Honey is part of agriculture, and it's a healthy substance for humans. Think of all the remedies that use honey. You can share the honey with your bees and use it to keep your daughter healthy. Although, I should note that honey isn't suitable for children under the age of one." His eyes crinkle at the edges. "Honey is powerful. It is after all, sweet to the soul and healthy for the body."

I feel a rush of gratitude to Barney for being kind about this. I can only guess how someone else might have reacted to my worrying about the morality of taking honey from bees.

"Okay." I nod and point to one of the objects in the box. "I know what that is. A smoker."

"Yes. It's filled with paper and lavender. I prefer lavender for the calming effect it has on the bees. I'll make sure to have Jack bring you some small plants from my garden, and you can grow some yourself." Barney picks up the smoker and hands it to me.

I smile at him. "Barney, you're a gift. I could never have done this without you."

He twinkles back. "Truthfully, I haven't felt this useful in a long time. Most people in this town think I'm blind and lame. No one asks me for advice anymore."

"I still can't believe someone started rumors about you being blind." I pick up a long, thin brush.

"People get bored." He shrugs and points to the tool in my hand. "That's used to brush the bees from the frames. The frames are where the bees store their honey."

"Okay." I place the brush back into the box. Grasping the hive tool firmly in one hand and holding onto the smoker in the other, I look at the hives.

"Alright. Show me what you know." Barney stands with his feet squarely planted. I finally notice he's not even wearing a bee suit. Standing next to him covered in a thick, tarp-like outfit with a huge, net-covered hat, I feel almost silly. Almost. I'm not about to take this thing off.

"Don't you need protection? What if they sting you?"

Barney waves a dismissive hand. "I've been stung before. But you're smoking the bees first, and most will be too sleepy to do anything. If you're gentle, no one will get stung."

I take a timid step forward, looking down at the hives. The one on the left has the least activity, so I reach for it.

Okay, Cordy. They're just bees. You've got the tools and the knowledge to at least open the hive.

Bolstered by my pep talk and Barney's unwavering gaze, I work at opening the hive. My smoker emits a pleasant smell, and I swear it's making me relax a little as well. Using the hive tool, I pry as gently as I can at the hive.

With a *crack,* it opens. Bees immediately crawl forward. For a second, I'm scared they'll fly at me, but I can see the smoke is doing its job. They're not aggressive; they're curious.

And they're actually kind of cute.

"Now, lift out a frame." Barney's calm voice reminds me of my purpose in opening the hive.

Now, I can see things that look like picture frames inside each section of the hive. There are eight frames in neat rows, each secured by little edges that allow me to pull one of the frames free. Using the thin brush, I gently bat a few bees back into the hive.

The frame is covered in thick, dark golden honey. I can identify honeycomb clinging to the frame. It's amazing, and the fresh, sweet smell makes my mouth water.

"Wow."

"It's beautiful, isn't it?" Barney murmurs behind me. I glance over my shoulder, and he grins a little. "Now it makes more sense why the land of milk and honey sounded so appealing, hm?"

"Yeah," I breathe. A few bees are venturing out of their hive. I need to finish this up before they get feisty. "Now what?"

"Jack?" Barney calls. Jack pauses in his game of peek-a-boo with Poppy and hurries over to place a large bucket and tea cloth down in front of Barney. "Place the frame in the bucket and cover it," Barney instructs. I do as he says.

We spend the next few minutes doing the same thing. Pulling out frames, inspecting them to see if there's enough honey to share, taking the ones that are full, and placing them in the covered bucket. Soon our bucket is full, and I crack open the last hive.

I'm surprised to find that this hive is not as vibrant as the first three. The frames are mostly empty, and the bees seem a little sluggish, even before I begin smoking them.

Pausing, I wave Barney over. "These bees look like they might be sick. Do bees get colds or something?"

Bending close to the hive, Barney examines the bees. Compared to the other hives, this one is almost empty, I realize. The bees don't look any different, but something is off.

Barney straightens. "Let's see what their queen looks like."

I eye the hive dubiously. "Where would she be?"

"She could be anywhere inside the hive, so this might take some time."

I glance back at the house. Poppy isn't going to last much longer. She may have Jack and Go-go to distract her, but that's not long enough to search a hive for a single bee.

"Let's get some lunch before we do that," I counter. "After I put Poppy down, we can look for the queen."

We don't find the queen. It turns out queens sometimes take off, leading most of the bees with them, but not all. I can't remember seeing the bees swarm, but Barney says it could have happened at any point, even if I was running errands or putting Poppy down for a nap.

The bees that are left have almost become . . . depressed? They don't know what to do anymore, and so they trundle around the hive looking for their queen, who has left them.

It's pretty sad, actually. Barney says he'll order me a new queen. I ask why they can't join one of the other hives, but I guess that's not how it works. For now, I'll mix up sugar water and take it to my sad hive until their new queen arrives. You know, to keep their spirits up. It's not needed, but I figure it might make them feel better about being left behind. I know that feeling all too well, and it's not fun.

It's weird how quickly my bees went from being a weird burden to being tiny, fuzzy, permanent fixtures in my life. I'm pretty worried about my little depressed hive. I try looking up online what to do about bee depression, but there isn't much out there. There isn't much to do besides replace the queen, which I'm now in the process of doing. And of course, my sugar-water syrup plan.

Barney and Jack leave, and I put Poppy down for the night. I sit playing with my extractor in one of the extra rooms downstairs. I've decided this room will be my honey room, which is pretty cool. I don't know anyone who has a room dedicated to honey.

Originally, I thought Jack looked like Santa, but it turns out Barney is my bee-related gift giver. Not only did he give me all of his old hive tools—which are in amazing condition, by the way—and his late wife's bee suit, but he's given me everything needed to harvest honey. Including the extractor.

It's basically a big barrel you set the frames in. There's a handle on the side that spins the barrel, and all the honey whooshes out of the frames. It eventually collects in the bottom of the barrel, where a little spigot lets the honey out.

My arm muscles burn after only spinning for a few minutes. Who knew I was so out of shape? But then again, it's not every day you use an extractor.

Finally, I take a break in my spinning, get a small mason jar, and place it under the tap. Then, holding my breath, I twist the little lever and wait.

Honey. Golden, slightly flaky honey drips out. The flakes are bits of beeswax, which are edible, according to a few of the books Barney gave me.

I've harvested honey. *Me.*

I dip my finger in the honey and try it. It's thick and sweet, and I feel an overwhelming sense of accomplishment. And then it hits me. I know what to do.

Chapter Seven
Ronan

Cordy's house looks great. Not to pat myself on the back or anything, but it looks great. Professional.

Which is saying something, because most of the carpentry work I've done prior to this was mending fences and building sheep barns. I did watch a *lot* of home improvement videos over the past few weeks. I even picked up a house-styling magazine to see some of the trends. I also did try to tell Cordy that her rustic exposed wood beams were hazardous, but she loves them. So we compromised, and I didn't touch them.

I shouldn't call them hazardous, but they do give the house an "I'm about to cave in" quality I usually like to avoid in homes.

Anyway, it's been two weeks since I came to fix the last broken window, and Cordy flew out her front door to meet me and tell me she finally had a plan. I'd been feeling a little disappointed. I only had one last thing to fix, but I'd already stalled for two weeks, and I couldn't do it anymore. I mean, it's a window, and it should have been fixed ages ago.

I was also getting tired of listening to Corwynn poke fun at how long it was taking me to fix Cordy's house. I didn't exactly tell him about how beautiful Cordy is. He thinks I'm a dodgy handyman.

But Cordy's new plan opened up the opportunity to keep hanging around. She's started a shop. Not a supermarket, but a little artisan shop that sells breads, cakes, honey products, tea, and other things.

It turns out one of her neighbors does knit, and Cordy is selling the knitting and taking forty percent of the profit. I told her it's usually the retailer who takes the larger cut, but she was adamant it wouldn't be fair.

The best part is, she doesn't need to rent a space, because I've transformed her living room area into a store. I'm quite proud of that.

The leaks have been fixed, and the area is open enough for a few small tables. Without the tarp covering the windows, sunlight gleams in, transforming the whole house into a cozy, sunny cottage. Compared to the grotty hovel I first took it to be, this is a much-needed step up.

I've not done it alone either. The floors have been buffed to an inch of their lives by Cordy, and she's set up all the tables to be easily accessible. Everything is in neat rows and has a neat price tag on as well.

Opening day is in three days, something Cordy hasn't stopped reminding me of. I finished the last touches—painting her baseboards—last night. Thus, I'm not needed at her home anymore, but I still find myself on her doorstep.

Not only because I want to be around her, but I'm also not getting anywhere with Corwynn. It's the summer holidays, so he's not exactly convinced he has to come back home. I have a little over a month to change his mind, but as of right now, I'd rather be knocking on the door of a beautiful, cheerful woman.

"Ronan!"

I love how her face lights up when she sees me.

I grin at her. "Good morning, love."

Cordy's kitchen is packed. Go-go is chasing a squealing Poppy around the table, and Cordy hurries back to the stove, spoon in hand. She's wearing an apron that's covered in flour and droplets of honey. There's a bit of flour on her nose too, I notice. She's never looked prettier.

"What are you doing here?" Cordy calls over the din of her daughter and goat.

"I came to see if you needed any help," I call back. "I know you're stressed about opening in a few days."

Pausing, she turns to survey me. "Okay," she says finally. "I'm sure you can tie a knot, right?"

Which is how I find myself tying clumps of herbs together with twine to hang from the dreaded exposed roof beams. Poppy comes around to inspect my handiwork and tries to pull a handful of purplish flowers off the table.

"Ah, no, Poppy." I shake my head at her. She frowns at me and reaches for the table again. I shift the herbs out of her reach and Poppy whines.

Cordy glances over from where she's now shaping loaves onto a baking tray and sighs. "You can't have them right now, baby."

"Here." I scoop Poppy onto my knee. "Can you help me?"

This cheers her up immensely. We work in something akin to harmony, Poppy passing me bits of twine and giving the strings a pull once I've started a knot.

"How's it going with you?" I ask Cordy. She's bent over the oven, setting the timer.

Straightening up, she blows hair out of her face and wipes her hands on her stained apron. "Well, there's enough bread in this house to feed an army of birds, and my non-perishables are all set up in the shop."

"But how're you feeling?"

"Like I might be sick."

"Then you're ready!" I clap my hands together. Poppy jumps and begins to cry.

Calmly, Cordy picks her daughter up and soothes her while I apologetically show Poppy it was only me. It only takes a few kisses and a biscuit for her to calm down. Cordy sets her on the kitchen floor, and Poppy toddles off to tease Go-go with her new treat.

Taking a seat across from me and grabbing one of the few bits of herbs, Cordy says, "And what about you and your brother?"

"We're . . . what's the saying? Ships in the night. I never see him, which I'm not sure how it's possible, given how small his flat is. He leaves before I wake up, and even if I stay up at night organizing coursework for next term, he still manages to come in after I sleep. If we do run into each other, he legs it to his room before I can get a word out. The only reason he hasn't kicked me out is he knows Mam would be furious, and he doesn't want to upset her or Da."

I finish the last bundle of herbs and shift the subject back to our task. "Where are these going?"

"Right here in the kitchen." Cordy stands and pulls a chair over to the sink. She climbs onto it and begins looping the twine around the beams over the sink. "I hope you two can talk soon."

I nod, not wanting to get back into Corwynn. If I'm being honest, I don't even know what to say to him. Instead, I keep the conversation focused on the shop and Cordy's worries. I might not be getting through to my brother, but I can at least be useful here.

Handing bundles of herbs up to Cordy, I feel at ease. There's something peaceful about this kitchen. The warm, yeasty smell of fresh bread, Cordy humming, and Poppy chasing Go-go around my legs feels right. This is how I imagined my life would be one day. Squealing children and all.

Chapter Eight
Cordy

The kitchen looks like a picture from a children's storybook.

The exposed beams I admired moving in are now housing drying herbs. They're part of my plan to sell loose leaf tea in the future. It's mostly lavender that Barney gave me, but I did find a wild mint plant, which I transplanted into my tiny herb garden. Vivian surprised me with a rosemary plant yesterday, but it's not quite big enough to harvest yet.

Jars of honey and jam are lined up on all the countertops. The jam is made from my neighbor's wild plum tree. It turns out the old lady a couple of doors up from me not only has wild plums in her backyard, but she's also killer at knitting. Agnes is selling some of her scarves, sweaters, and shawls in my shop.

I don't have a proper name for my new business yet. I toyed with "The Bee's Knees," but Ronan nearly laughed me out of the kitchen. So I'm calling it The Corner Shop for now. It'll have to do.

The shop isn't much, but it's all I've got. And I'm proud. I already have plans to use goat's milk to make soap and other body products once Go-go can produce milk. It'll be next year, but it feels nice to have a plan.

I've blinked, and now we're officially opening in an hour. An hour! Ronan is already here, steady and smiling. He had the idea to sell coffee, and was willing to let me borrow his French press, but I felt like I'd be taking Vivian's customers away. So we're saving the coffee idea for later.

Overall, I think the shop has a good chance of not failing.

Ronan comes up beside me and hands me a cup of my coffee. "Are you ready?"

"I think so." I survey the living room, transformed into a rustic, homey shop.

All my baked goods are lined up neatly in their clear-plastic packaging. I nervously shift some of the small cases of lavender shortbread cookies and step back to assess their symmetry. The rustic twine tied around the cookies gives me a twinge of pride. Even though it's simple, the food looks lovely.

I have Vivian to thank for that. I went to her two weeks ago and asked if I could have some food packaging supplies. I did some budgeting, and I decided that if I didn't want this to fail, I would have to put up a little of my carefully hoarded money. I was terrified to use it because I have no prospect of a job, but now . . . well, it feels like I need to risk a little. I hope it works out.

Vivian, because she's the sweetest person alive, took only half of the money. She told me to consider it a down payment, but not to worry about getting her the second half until I'm on my feet. I almost cried as I took my supplies back home.

"Well I hope so, because here's your first customer." Ronan's words snap me back to reality.

Nervously, I smile at Agnes as she trundles in. *We've got this.*

It's a roaring success.

Well, as roaring as Arbury can be. Vivian stopped by and bought four jars of honey. Jack brought Barney, and both of them bought a couple of loaves of bread, honey, and wild plum jam. A few neighbors who I haven't officially met came by too, and overall, it felt busy and exciting.

It's not as if I can retire, but I had fun and I did make some money. Everyone who came by acted as if they were excited about the prospect of a little artisan shop, so I hope the enthusiasm keeps up.

Ronan stayed the whole time and helped keep Go-go off the tables. This turned out to be a surprisingly big problem, but Go-go is such a novelty that most people thought she was adorable. She did scare a little old lady who turned out to be Vivian's mother, but Mrs. Woodhouse recovered herself well. She even said she'd come back tomorrow and bring her knitting club.

Poppy snuggles into my shoulder as I close up. Bringing the two loaves that weren't sold into the kitchen, I find Ronan making coffee.

"Oh! I thought you went home." I place the loaves on the table.

"I thought you'd like a cup of coffee after your long day." Ronan smiles easily. "And we need to celebrate your first day as an independent woman."

Poppy reaches for the cup Ronan hands me, and I gently shift her onto my hip to get her little hands out of reach. Taking the cup from Ronan, I take a sip. Then, trying not to gag, I set the mug back down.

"Too strong?" Ronan laughs.

Man, he has the best laugh.

"A little." I grin. "Do you want to stay for dinner? Pops is pretty hungry." Go-go bleats from the floor, and I laugh. "Go-go too, apparently."

"I'll help," Ronan says, and I swear it's one of the most attractive things a man has ever said to me.

Poppy is in bed and Go-go sleepily chews her cud in the corner of the kitchen as Ronan helps me clean up the mess of spaghetti from

Poppy's highchair. I can't help but admire him as he washes the plates. How can a person be attractive while washing dishes?

I'm going to have to splash some cold water on my face if this line of thinking keeps up. I'm practically drooling over the guy, who hasn't shown much interest in me romantically. I mean, he has been coming to my house every day for over a month, but he's never sent me any real signals. No lingering looks or touches, no outright flirtatious comments, nothing. He just comes, works on my house, brings us food, and leaves. Not a terrible relationship, really, but one that would be better with a few stray kisses here and there. Or a lot of stray kisses.

As if he's heard my thoughts, Ronan turns to look at me. "Any more?"

It takes me a second to realize he's asking if there are any more dishes. I shake my head. "I think you got them all."

"Great. Well, I suppose I should head out. Take another stab at convincing my brother he needs to go home. I'm hoping he'll go back to Mam's to take his last exams next week."

"That's soon." I try to keep the disappointment out of my voice. *Stop it, Cordy. You're not even dating him.*

"Knowing my brother, I doubt he'll go for it." Ronan shrugs and smiles a little.

He comes around the table and stands in front of me. It's not inappropriate so far. We're just talking.

Except . . . it feels like a magnet is tugging me closer, and I take another step, trying to appear casual. "Thanks so much for helping today. You have no idea how much it meant to me."

"You did great today." Ronan beams down at me. His obvious pride in me draws me closer. I can't remember the last time someone looked this proud of me. Somehow we're only inches apart now. "You've got a good chance of this being the new shop in town. I bet tourists would even come in."

The thought of people specifically coming to Arbury to see The Corner Shop makes me a little queasy. I mean, talk about pressure. Except, that would be super cool too.

"You think so?"

"Don't look so nervous." He laughs. "That would be a good thing."

Okay, he definitely just looked at my mouth. Not as if I haven't been glancing at his.

"Thank you." My voice comes out a little huskier than I intend. I clear my throat and he raises an eyebrow at me. "You've done a lot for me and for Poppy. Honestly, I probably couldn't have pulled this off without you. The whole shop setup would have taken forever without your help."

He winks. "Ay, I'm glad to be useful."

"You've been more than useful! If this shop makes it, you will have saved me from working some desk job that I would hate. This has been wonderful."

Grabbing his hand, I squeeze it. I need him to know how thankful I am, and I'm not sure I'm doing a good job expressing myself under the circumstances. The circumstances being that I can't stop thinking about what it would be like to kiss him.

He turns my hand over and rubs circles into my palm with his thumb. "Can I tell you something?" When I nod, he continues. "I've been thinking about kissing you ever since we met. I didn't want to cross any boundaries, especially in front of Poppy, but . . ." I feel a rush of warmth toward him as he trails off.

He's looking so endearingly at me that I lean in, stopping only a few inches from him. This is happening. I try to remember the last time I brushed my teeth. That would be a heck of a first kiss to have food in my teeth, and I'm ninety percent sure I'm about to kiss Ronan Thomson. His eyes flick down to my mouth again and he reaches up to cup my cheek.

I'm going to kiss him.

And then I don't. Poppy makes a squealing yell from the other room, and on instinct, I turn toward her voice. For a second, we stand frozen, both of us waiting for Poppy to make another sound. I'm met with silence from the other room. Then I remember what we were about to do.

"Sorry. We moms are hardwired to respond to baby cries," I say a little ruefully, turning back to Ronan.

He takes a step back and laughs. "Do you want to check on her?"

"Yes." I give him a little grin as I walk quietly out of the kitchen.

I've not been on a date since Poppy's dad and I split up, so I'm not sure if most men would have been annoyed by Poppy's interruption. Clearly, Ronan has been thinking about my daughter since the start, and it's incredibly soul-warming that he's fine with me being a mom first, a date second. Not that this is a date.

It would be a red flag if he wasn't okay with me being a mom first, I realize as I look down at Poppy snoozing peacefully. She must have had a dream or couldn't roll over the way she wanted to. I stare at her sleeping face for a moment as guilt crashes over me. I have to think of her when it comes to dating, to bringing anyone new into her life. Am I ready to do that? Is Ronan the kind of guy I want in Poppy's life?

Suddenly, I'm grateful for her little shout. Because if I'm being honest, have I really thought about what dating someone would mean? I want to, I do. I want to go kiss Ronan and see what his beard feels like against my skin, but . . . am I ready? Is she ready?

"I won't let anyone into your life who is bad for you. Or me," I whisper to Poppy, gripping the side of her crib.

Walking back downstairs, I decide I'm going to have to move slowly with Ronan. I can't let some cute guy sweep me off my feet without considering Poppy. There's more at stake here besides my heart.

Chapter Nine
Cordy

"Happy birthday to you! Happy birthday, dear Poppy! Happy birthday to you!"

The kitchen bursts into applause, and Poppy beams at us from her highchair, watching as I set the tiny chocolate cake in front of her. With a squeal, she smashes both hands into the cake. Go-go jumps beside her, waiting for a taste. That goat has gotten fat from all the snacks Poppy has been sharing with her.

Vivian laughs as she takes pictures for both of us. "It's a good thing you made us a cake too." She's turned out to be a good friend, Vivian. Her mother even comes by the shop most days, although she keeps a wary eye on Go-go the whole time she's here.

My enthusiastic daughter sprays chocolate crumbs across the kitchen. I'll worry about cleaning it up later. Vivian begins handing out plates of the lavender honey cake I made for the adults. "Which, by the way, is great."

"It's a new recipe I'm trying." I accept a plate from her.

"Cordy, you're tipping me, hon."

I lift my phone so Mom, who is video calling, can celebrate her granddaughter turning one.

"Sorry, Mom."

As everyone digs into their cake, I smile around at the people who've come. Barney and Jack are here, and Jack's brought his wife, who is the most Mrs. Claus person I've ever met. She immediately swept me into a hug and said Poppy and I should both call her "Gran."

And Ronan is here.

We haven't kissed. When I got back from checking on Poppy that night two weeks ago, I told him I had to be very sure about who I was bringing into Poppy's life. And because he's Ronan, he was kind, understanding, and reasonable. Which made me want to kiss him even more, but I did a good job restraining myself.

He stopped coming around so much after that, but it's because he's been full-force trying to talk to his brother. Last night he came by to help me set up Poppy's party, and apologize for being MIA. Then he asked me out.

"On a proper date. We can talk and get to know each other." He looked so cute that I couldn't have said no, even if I wasn't dying for him to ask me. "I want to be able to kiss you in the foreseeable future, Cordy Brown," he added with a wink.

So basically, I've been thinking nonstop about what a date with Ronan would be like.

"Cordelia Mae, you're tipping me." Mom's voice breaks through my Ronan-haze.

"Sorry, Mom." I adjust the phone so she can see Poppy cramming cake into her mouth.

"Did you get my present?" Mom asks for the third time today.

I sigh. "Yes, Mom. I told you already. Hang on, let me get it."

"Well, you can give me a tour while you're at it," she says as I head into the living room. "I still haven't seen your house."

That's because it was a swamp when we moved in, and I didn't want my mother to have a stroke and then lecture me for days about how I should move home. I love her, but sometimes she can be a little much.

"Sure." I switch my camera around so she can see my mini shop. "This is the store."

Mom doesn't say anything right away, and I feel a flicker of irritation. She knows how much effort I put into this space. She also knows it's been going pretty well. I mean, it's not been that long since I opened, but I've had a steady stream of customers. And I have ideas to expand. Like finding a farmers' market and setting up shop there as well.

"I have it set up so people can flow around the room." Mom's still not said anything.

"It's very . . . quaint," she finally ventures. I roll my eyes.

Okay. I'm probably a little oversensitive when it comes to my shop, but it's because I have *nothing* else. If I didn't have this, I'd be caving to Mom's offer of a plane ticket home. I want to succeed on my own. Is that so hard to fathom?

A knock at the door saves my mom from coming up with other forced compliments and saves me from grinding my teeth to a pulp.

"Hang on, Mom." I switch the camera back on my phone so she can see my face instead of the floor as I answer the door. "Hello?"

"Good morning." The older man on the other side of my door nods stiffly. "I was told this is the place to buy honey."

I blink in surprise. Someone actually sent this man to me for honey? I feel a little bit like a celebrity. "Oh, well sure!" I nudge the door a little wider. "I'm technically closed today, but if you just need a jar of honey . . ."

I trail off as I hurry to my honey table. What perfect timing too. Now Mom can see the store isn't a flop and I'm not in desperate need of saving. When I turn around to hand the honey to the man, I find him gaping around my living room. Again, I get a spark of satisfaction. This would have been a better reaction from Mom.

"It's nice, isn't it?" I can't help but say. "My friend Ronan helped me set this all up. He found all sorts of odds and ends, and it all seems to fit together."

"Is this a shop?" The man's voice is hard to read.

"Yes, albeit a pretty new one. I opened a couple of weeks ago."

It's then I notice he doesn't look impressed or pleased by this information. In fact, he looks horrified.

"You're running a shop from your home?"

I'm acutely aware that not only is my mother listening to this trainwreck of a conversation, but Ronan and Vivian have now appeared in the kitchen door. Poppy toddles across the room to me, clutching her stuffed pony. Reaching me, she wraps her arms around my knees and watches the newcomer with round eyes.

"Um, yes." I fiddle nervously with a lock of Poppy's hair.

On cue, Go-go bounds into the room. I swear my heart stops. I've been pretty good at keeping Go-go out of my shop and contained to the kitchen. Mostly because of poor Mrs. Woodhouse, but also because she is an animal and this is a shop. But apparently, Go-go has recognized this as her opportunity to be involved.

As I reach for her, she makes a flying leap onto my honey display. With a crash, two jars of honey fall.

Oh no. Oh, please no.

"Is . . . is that a goat?" The man has gone completely white.

"I . . . I . . ." The words aren't coming out. Go-go just smashed two jars' worth of honey and is prancing around my shop of mostly edible things like a demented ballerina. This violates at least three different health codes.

Ronan steps forward and quickly gathers Go-go in his arms. She makes a deep-throated sound that draws everyone's eyes to her. This could not be going worse.

"Go-go!" Poppy shrieks, lurching forward to grab at her beloved pet. She trips over a wrinkle in the rug that Go-go managed to make as she was galloping around the room.

It all happens in slow motion. Poppy falling forward, Go-go jerking out of Ronan's arms, Vivian reaching for Poppy at the same time as I do, and the old man gaping at us.

A crash sounds at the same time I manage to catch Poppy's head before she hits the tiled floor. It's an awkward hold, my hands half cradling her face while I try to grab her body as well. Straightening, I knock heads with Vivian, and both of us hiss in suppressed pain.

A strong hand helps me up, Poppy in my arms, and I give Ronan a quick, thankful smile.

Then I survey the damage. My daughter is fine. She's wide-eyed but grinning as she takes in the mess before her. Because it is a horrible mess.

In her attempt to break free of Ronan, Go-go has jumped back onto the honey table. I'm not sure if it was the slippery edge of the table coupled with her hooves, or just plain bad aim, but my ten-pound baby goat has knocked all the other honey jars to the floor.

Every single one.

I want to cry. All that work. All that time spinning the honey out of the frames and painstakingly collecting it into jars. All that time hand-making labels. It's all gone.

A clearing throat makes me turn. The old man is glaring at me, his left eye twitching ever so slightly. "Do you have the proper business registration for this . . . establishment?"

His icy words bounce around my mind, but I don't grasp what he's saying. Then I remember the online form I filled out back when I realized I could pull this off. "Yes, I do."

The man holds out a hand. "May I see it?"

"Why?" It's Ronan who steps forward. It almost looks like he's squaring off with the smaller man.

With narrowed eyes, the man says, "I'm Harold Smith. I used to be a health inspector until I retired last year. It's my business to see if this is a legal establishment."

I wish he'd stop calling this "an establishment." What's wrong with the word "shop"?

"If you're retired, I don't reckon it is your business." Ronan folds his arms firmly across his chest and stares down Harold Smith.

"Ronan." I place a hand on his arm. "I can get the form."

"You don't have to cave to this man's bullying, Cordy." Ronan turns to me, and I can see the concern and protectiveness in his eyes.

"Bully!" Harold Smith splutters.

Ronan spins on him, but Vivian steps in. "I'm sorry, Mr. Smith, but this is actually a birthday party, so if you'd like to come back and further discuss this, please do so on Monday."

Bless Vivian. Harold Smith glares at her, but he turns to leave, handing Ronan the jar of honey he'd been grasping. The only jar of honey I currently have in stock.

The door slams shut behind him. Poppy jumps a little in my arms. She's already trying to get down and play, but there are glass shards all over the floor.

"I'll get a broom," Vivian volunteers.

"All that honey," Barney whispers. His face is creased with so much disappointment that I feel a pang of guilt.

"It's all right, Cordy. We'll get it sorted," Ronan says firmly.

Barney straightens up. "Of course we will."

"Yes, why don't you take the birthday girl and Go-go to the bedroom and let us clean this up?" Vivian shoos us out of the living room.

Closing the bedroom door behind me, I let Poppy down and watch her scamper with Go-go onto the bed. What on earth am I going to do?

"Well, that was a disaster." Mom's voice comes from my phone, which I realize I'm somehow still clutching.

Of course she would witness that.

"But," Mom continues, "it'll work itself out. He's not even a health inspector anymore."

"Thanks, Mom." I'm a little bolstered by her surprisingly optimistic opinion.

"Oh, and Cordy, don't forget my present."

Chapter Ten
Ronan

"I'm glad Poppy won't remember any of this." Cordy takes a gulp of coffee. "What a disaster."

"It wasn't that bad," I say, then immediately regret it.

Cordy's eyes fill with tears. "Not that bad? Ronan, a goat destroyed all the honey I had to sell. In front of an ex-health inspector, who is definitely holding a grudge. Also, I don't know if I can harvest more honey or not. What am I going to do?"

Scrambling to think of something, I shift my chair closer to her. "But for Poppy, it was a lovely day. She had cake and presents. She got to be around people she loves. It may have been a rubbish day for you, but if you're worried about her, don't be."

She's silent for a moment, then turns to look up at me. Her eyes still brim with tears, and she blinks rapidly to clear them away. She's chewing on her full bottom lip, and I can see she's irritated the skin enough to cause a raw spot to appear.

I have the urge to kiss her.

"You think so?"

It takes me a second to remember what I just said to her. "Yes. Poppy had a great day. I'm sorry that Harold guy was rude."

"Well, I did have a goat in my shop." Cordy grimaces. "Thanks for hanging out with me and letting me complain." She attempts a laugh that comes out hollow.

"Always." I grab her hand and smooth my thumb over her knuckles.

She shifts forward in her seat, closer to me. Again, I glance down at her mouth.

Get a grip, Ronan. We're taking it slow.

"I'd like to have that date soon." She sounds almost shy.

I grin at her. "Me too."

"Can this count as a half date?" She raises an eyebrow at me questioningly.

"Do I get half a kiss at the end?" I joke.

Cordy laughs and settles back into her seat. "Maybe I'll give you a peck on the cheek."

"I'll take it." I laugh too. "What do people do on a half date?"

She pauses to think for a moment before saying, "They ask each other one serious and one silly question, then they eat chocolate and talk about something like how to house train goats."

I nod. "That sounds about right. Shall I go first?"

"Only if you start with the silly question first."

"Okay, what's your most controversial food preference?"

She eyes me for a long second. "You'll judge me."

"I won't."

"You will. Everyone does."

I reach out and tug on a strand of her hair. "Cordy Brown, I can promise I won't judge you on your horrible food preference."

"Okay. I like mayo on apples." She peeks at me through her eyelashes.

I stare. "I take it back. That's weird. Mayonnaise with apples?"

"Oh, yeah. Have you never tried it?"

The effort to keep the grimace off my face is killing me. "I can't say I've tried that particular type of combination."

She bursts out laughing. "I'm kidding. I couldn't eat that. No, my controversial food opinion is that I don't like bacon. It's weird and tastes too much like . . . pigs."

It's my turn to laugh. "If I remember correctly, bacon comes from pigs."

She smacks my arm. "No, really, it tastes almost like the pigs are still alive." I'm still laughing when she asks, "What's your favorite type of candy?"

"Starbursts," I say immediately.

"Which color is the best?"

"Red."

"Red? That's crazy. Pink is the best."

She's laughing again, and I take a second to listen to her laugh echo in the kitchen. I could get used to this life.

"Okay, now I can ask you a serious question." I bring her back to her game. She grins at me, but I'm guessing her smile is about to fade. "What's up with you and your mam? I see how stressed you get when she calls you."

Just as I guessed, her smile slips a little. "Oh. Well, she really wants me to move back to South Carolina, and I really don't. Mom isn't the kind of person to let things go. She likes to win. And for my part, I'm not caving."

"Why does she want you to move back?"

She shrugs and looks away. "It's sort of complicated. It's always been me and Mom. My dad died when I was three, so I never got to know him very well. Mom has done a great job raising me by herself, but she did start to get . . . worried about me. She didn't want me to go anywhere or do anything, and then I got it into my head to go to England."

"Why England?" I watch a slight, dreamy smile cross her face.

"There was always something about England. I'm not even sure what lured me in, but I fell in love. I desperately wanted to come here, and that . . . well, I think coming here may have broken my mom's heart a little. It's not as if she's alone. She has her best friend and her sister, but I know that's not the same. Unfortunately, Mom started getting pretty passive-aggressive about me being in England, and it kind of deepened the wedge between us. I guess I started the wedge, but she's not helping." She finishes her explanation in a whisper.

"I'm sorry, Cordy." I reach out to touch her hand. "Have you tried talking to your mam?"

She frowns. "I think so. Well, I tried once, but I'm not sure we were ready for that conversation. It's very awkward, and neither of us is great with awkward conversations."

We fall into silence, Cordy biting her lip and staring at her hands.

"Hey, I'm sorry." I squeeze her hand. "I didn't think about how that question might have been loaded. I'm not sure what I was thinking. I shouldn't have asked."

She shakes her head and gives a quick smile. "No, it's okay. You couldn't have known. Plenty of people have strained relationships with their moms, so it's not an unusual question."

"If it makes you feel better, you can ask me a heavy family question."

"Okay." Her smile comes back a little. "Tell me about your brother."

I groan. "Okay, that's fair. Alright, Corwynn and I have a strained relationship as well."

"Wait. Corwynn? Does he work on a farm?" She frowns at me.

"Yeah, how did you know?" For a second, I picture her and Corwynn on a date. Which is ridiculous, because Corwynn is a minor and Cordy wouldn't date someone right now anyway.

"He's the jerk who beat me out of the job that I told you about." Cordy laughs. "I didn't realize that you are his brother."

"He is a bit of a jerk." I chuckle. Then I say more soberly, "We've had a tough time the last few years."

"Why?" Cordy fixes her blue eyes on me, and I feel the knee-jerk tension that always floods me when I talk about Corwynn relaxing. If she can get me to relax while talking about Corwynn, she must be the one for me.

"I'm twelve years older than Corwynn, and he and I never clicked. I was more interested in girls and hanging out with my mates than I was in being with him. Our age gap always made it feel like babysitting, but now I can see he just wanted to be around his older brother. He's always felt like I don't love him, but that's clearly not true. I'm not sure how to show him that I do."

"And you came down here to bring him home?"

"Yeah, he didn't want to deal with his life anymore. He didn't want to take his exams and get a proper job, nor does he apparently want to take over the family farm. It's beyond me why he left one farm to come work for another."

Cordy laces her fingers through mine. "Did you ask him why he left?"

I pull up short, but then shake my head. "He left because he feels like Mam loves him less than she loves . . . well, me, I guess. He's always been more dramatic than me."

"Is that what he said?"

"No, not in so many words." I frown down at her.

She raises an eyebrow. "Why don't you ask him why he left?" I open my mouth to tell her it doesn't matter when she continues, "And I doubt it was the farm that made him run away. He obviously doesn't hate farming if he's willing to work for Jack. He just wants to do the work on his terms."

"His terms? What terms? He's seventeen. He doesn't have—"

She interrupts me gently, squeezing my hand. "Try talking to him. He has a reason for what he's done."

Trying not to let my exasperation show, I squeeze her hand back. "I've tried talking to him, but he doesn't want to listen."

"Maybe you need to do the listening."

We fall into silence, and I absorb her words. Haven't I been listening? Thinking back on our conversations, I can see I haven't tried very hard to find out why Corwynn left.

"I'm not sure where to start," I finally say.

Her eyes crinkle, and she winks. "Maybe spend more time with him. You know how much I like seeing you every day, but Corwynn might see it as you once again hanging out with 'a girl' instead of him."

Even though she's spoken lightly and even tried to be playful about it, her words smack me in the chest. I pull my hand back, stung by her words. I'm not sure if I'm angry with her for pointing out the pattern, or angry at myself for falling back into the same behavior from when Corwynn and I were kids.

Slowly, I stand up from the table. "I better get going."

Cordy bites her lip again. "I'm not trying to make you feel bad. I'm . . . I don't want you to have a bad relationship with your brother."

"We're fine." I know my tone is short, and I see her wince.

She's trying to help, Ronan.

I sigh, blowing out as much tension as I can. "I'm sorry. I know you're trying to help. I need to think." I lean in to kiss her cheek. Even in my disgruntled state, I notice that she smells faintly of something sweet and warm. "I'm sorry."

"Don't be sorry." She shakes her head.

"Now we know the two silly and two serious questions game is a little too heavy for a half date." I smile at her. The tension finally breaks when she laughs.

"I should have known. Well, I won't suggest it on our actual date if you won't." She searches my face.

"That sounds like a good plan. I'd prefer for our actual date to end with a real kiss and not me being an eejit."

Her eyes sparkle. "I'd like that very much." She brushes a hand across her cheek where I kissed her before standing up. "Now go see your brother and spend tomorrow with him. I don't want to see you in this shop." She puts on a mock stern voice.

Laughing, I let her shepherd me to the door. At the threshold, I turn to look at her. "Forgive me for getting short with you?"

"Of course." She smiles.

"Goodnight, Cordy."

"Goodnight, Ronan." She shoots me one last smile before gently pushing me out the door. As her hand leaves my chest and the door closes, I fight the urge to pull her into my arms. Instead, I get to go have a conversation with a man about a rat.

Chapter Eleven
Cordy

The bell I installed over my front door tinkles merrily as a new customer comes in. I'm filling the honey table with the last few jars I'd saved for myself, and finish my task before turning. I have plans to try to extract more honey this weekend, but for now, this will have to do.

In an attempt to keep my tables full, I spent all day yesterday baking bread, muffins, and cookies. Some of my herbs finally reached a good drying point too, so I have some lavender shortbread and rosemary bread, as well as small jars of dried herbs and a few tea mixes. The shop looks pretty good, even with the glaring absence of my usual honey.

"Good morning." I turn to greet my customer and come to a stop. It's Harold Smith.

He looks just as unpleasant as the last time we spoke. He eyes the shop before staring at me. "Are there any rogue goats in here today?"

Jack came over yesterday morning and helped me put together a little pen in the backyard for Go-go. I didn't want her to get into the bees—or the shop—and that's where she is now. Not that I appreciate Harold Smith's tone.

"How can I help you, Mr. Smith?"

"I know you have no legal obligation to show me your credentials, Ms. . . ."

"Ms. Brown."

"Yes." Harold clears his throat. "As I was saying, you do not need to prove anything to me legally, but if there were a licensed health inspector, you'd be subject to his or her authority."

Okay, I can't stand this guy. He makes it sound like I'm some horrible woman who spit in his tea.

"I suppose I would," I concede.

The smirk that flickers across Harold's mouth puts me on edge. I assume he's called some health inspector friend in, but I can't be in much trouble. I put Go-go up, I am licensed, and I have a right to this shop. It's my own house, for crying out loud!

"Well, my colleague will be coming around any minute. I'll take my leave." Harold turns toward the door as I stare at him. He came all this way to tell me he ratted me out and isn't even going to stay?

"Former colleague," I find myself saying.

The tips of Harold's ears redden, but he doesn't turn. "Good day, Ms. Brown."

The door swings shut, the bells chiming cheerily again. I can't believe the nerve of that guy. It was just a goat. If I have a pet goat in my home on a day when my shop is closed, who is to tell me I'm in the wrong?

Apparently Harold freaking Smith.

A knock at the door makes me stiffen. This has to be the actual inspector. With a sigh, I cross the room. Pulling open the door, I plaster a smile onto my face only to have it fall off immediately.

Malcolm?

It is Malcolm. Malcolm Carmichael II is standing on my front step. He looks as shocked to see me as I am to see him.

"Cordelia?" He gapes at me. His eyes scan up and then down my body, as if he's trying to make sure I'm not a horse wearing a Cordy Brown mask.

"Malcolm? You're a health inspector?" I sputter.

"You have a pet goat?" He sounds absolutely flummoxed.

"I refuse to have you as an inspector." Ignoring his question, I fold my arms across my chest and glare at him.

"Cordelia . . ." he wheedles.

"What, Malcolm? You think I want to work with you after—"

A perfectly timed shout from Poppy, who is supposed to be napping, pulls me up short. On instinct, I turn away from Malcolm and go to get her. I need a breather anyway.

I take two steps when I realize I'm not sure I want Malcolm to meet Poppy. Coming to a stop, I try to process my next step. Apparently sensing my hesitation, Poppy shouts louder.

"Mama!"

"Cordelia?"

I turn to meet Malcolm's gaze.

"Is that . . .?"

"That's your daughter, yes."

The ice in my voice makes Malcolm flinch. Or maybe he flinched because the consequences of his actions have finally caught up with him. They always do.

Recovering himself, Malcolm takes a step inside and shuts the door behind him. "Can I meet her?" Then seeing my face, he adds, "Please."

He does look like he's, at the minimum, interested in meeting Poppy. I'm sure the internal battle that's currently taking place is all over my face.

When Poppy shouts my name again, I cave. If Poppy were older, I would probably kick Malcolm out, but she won't remember this or remember if he disappears from our lives again. At least I hope she won't.

"Fine. But you're on thin ice."

Malcolm nods hard and shuffles uncomfortably. I leave him to get Poppy.

I'm greeted with a squeal as Poppy hangs on the edge of her crib. Her big blue eyes crinkle as she grins her little gap-toothed smile. "Mama!"

"Hey, baby." I scoop her up and snuggle a kiss into her neck. She giggles loudly and places an open-mouth kiss on my cheek. Those are my favorite kinds of kisses.

Between kisses and tickles, I change her diaper and tug her soft purple onesie over her head. Her baby hair sticks up endearingly, and I smooth my hand over her head.

Okay, I'm stalling. But it's because I'm not sure this is the best idea. I mean, Malcolm ghosted me *the second* he found out I was pregnant. He can't waltz back into my life unannounced. Or into Poppy's life.

Here I've been keeping Ronan at arm's length, worried he'll somehow disrupt Poppy's life, and now I'm letting Malcolm meet her?

"Stop it, Cordy. He's just seeing her. He's not moving in or even asking for playdates. I can set up as many boundaries as I need." With a sigh, I pick up Poppy. "Let's do this, Pops." She blows a raspberry. "That's right, baby. That's how I feel too," I murmur.

I watch Malcolm, trying to see any hint of a negative emotion cross his face. While he looks a little shell-shocked, he also looks . . . interested. He's interested in meeting Poppy. The ice around my heart melts a little.

"I'm embarrassed to ask this, but what's her name?" Malcolm doesn't take his eyes off Poppy. She grins at him widely, and I can starkly see she has similar features to her father. Something about her smile reminds me of him, now that I'm comparing.

"Poppy. Poppy Elise Brown."

"Ah." Malcolm glances at me but then quickly back to Poppy.

I bristle. What, does he not like her name? Well, if he wanted an opinion, he should have stuck around, shouldn't he? How dare he turn up his nose at anything regarding my little girl!

"What, Malcolm?" The ice has frozen around my heart again.

"She has your last name," he says, looking a little sheepish.

I'm taken aback. "Of course she has my last name. Why wouldn't she? You left us, remember?"

Malcolm turns brick red. "I didn't . . . I hadn't . . . I thought you were lying."

I gape at him. "Lying? About being pregnant?"

He has the grace to look ashamed. "Yes."

"Why on earth would I lie about something like that?"

"I thought . . ." He trails off, frowning at the floor.

Setting Poppy down so she can begin her normal exploration, I fold my arms tightly across my chest. "What did you think, Malcolm?"

"I thought you were trying to get me to marry you," he says almost too quietly for me to hear.

I laugh. All those nights I spent wondering why Malcolm left me and wondering why he'd transferred universities, I hadn't thought this. And even if I had wanted to marry him, was the thought of marrying me so hideous to him that he would flee?

"I never said I wanted to get married to you when I called to tell you, Malcolm. I mean, I did. I thought we could get married and start a little family, but I didn't tell you that when I called you. All I said was I was pregnant. Why did you think it was a plot to get you to marry me?" I watch his face for any hint of motivation. He stares at me like I'm the demented one.

After taking a deep breath, he frowns at me. "For the money, Cordelia."

"What money? Malcolm, what are you talking about?" I want to shake sense out of him. I never imagined this conversation going this way.

He's still looking at me like I'm the crazy one. "My family's money. I thought you were trying to get me to marry you so you could be part of the Carmichael estate. It's happened before, you know," he adds with a quick shrug. "Women like money."

I ignore his last statement and grasp at the part of his story that doesn't make sense. "Your family is rich?"

"Of course, Cordelia. Are you trying to convince me you didn't know?"

I throw up my hands in exasperation. "I didn't!"

"You did."

"Malcolm. How would I know that you were some Richie Richerson? All my friends were on scholarships, just like me, and you hung out with them. I've never once heard you mention your parents' money. You never told me you had money. We almost always ate takeout. Do you want me to go on?"

"I told you my dad owns Happy Duck Shortbread."

"Duck?" Poppy toddles over to Malcolm, her blue eyes large. "Quack!" she adds with enthusiasm.

Some of the tension in my neck eases and I take a moment to breathe. Poppy is the cutest tension breaker I've ever met. She holds her arms up to Malcolm, and I notice immediately that he doesn't seem thrilled by the prospect of picking her up.

Instead, he pats her on the head and makes a shushing sound. I bite back the urge to snap at him that she isn't a dog.

"Come here, baby," I say to her, holding out my arms. Poppy abandons Malcolm cheerfully to come to me. I scoop her up and turn my attention back to the problem in front of me.

"Malcolm. You said your dad *worked* at Happy Duck Shortbread. You didn't say he owned the largest cookie company in England."

"Second largest."

"What?"

Malcolm clears his throat. "Second largest. Sugargo is still making higher sales than us."

"That's hardly the point right now." I scowl at him. "You didn't even ask me about my pregnancy and if I was lying. You didn't even come with me to the first appointment, which, by the way, would have cleared all of this up. You didn't give me a chance before disappearing and *transferring schools*! Who does that? Your first impulse was to run away from me, and you went with that impulse."

The pink tinge in Malcolm's cheeks darkens. "Cordelia, I didn't know—"

"Yes. You didn't know." I hoist Poppy higher onto my hip to make my point. "You had no idea this beautiful little girl existed. You have no idea what her favorite snack is, or how many words she can say. You don't know when her birthday is, or if she has ever been in the hospital. You don't know what her laugh sounds like. You. Don't. Know. Because you left without talking to me. You don't know anything about your own daughter, because you thought I was some gold-digging trollop, even though I never once asked you for money and I was perfectly happy eating cheap Chinese food with you every weekend." I'm breathing hard when I finish. I want to cry, but that wouldn't help anything at this point. "And you know what? Now that I do know you're part of the elite that you and I used to poke fun at for their sports coats and snubbed noses, I still don't want any money from you."

"Cordelia." Malcolm frowns at me. "Be reasonable. Of course I'll set up a trust fund for Poppy. She shouldn't go without because you hate me."

His business-like demeanor enrages me. Rage seems like a strong word until you're faced with someone you used to love talking to you as if you're a petulant child. I'm the unreasonable one? After how he handled the news about being a father? No.

"I don't hate you. I'm saying I'm not going to be asking for money from you. I don't care if you set up something for Poppy, but you have no obligation to do so." Poppy wriggles in my arms and I set her down.

"Of course I do. I'm her father!" A tight silence follows his words, and we both look at each other. Then slowly, his eyes grow wider. "Am I her father?"

I throw up my hands in pure irritation. "Yes, Malcolm. You are her father. But I didn't put your name on her birth certificate, so legally you have no ties to her."

He looks as if I've hit him. "Why would you do that?"

"Oh, gee, Malcolm, I don't know. Maybe because you *transferred universities to get away from us*."

"But . . . but I'm her father." He turns to look at Poppy, who has found one of her stuffed animals and is waving it around as she toddles about.

"You've not acted like a father." Even I know the words are harsh as they come out. I sigh, ready to apologize for at least being callous, but Malcolm looks back at me, and I can see he understands.

"Why didn't you tell me after she was born?"

I think about his question for a moment. "Because she was all mine. I did everything, and I didn't want to share her birth with you after . . . well, you know. Then as the months went by, I wanted less and less to share her with you. I didn't feel like you deserved her."

"And you didn't think she'd want to meet me someday?" Malcolm's voice hints at an accusation, and I bristle.

"That would have been her choice, Malcolm. I would have helped her find you."

"So you kept her from me because you're holding a grudge." His tone is flat.

"Look, I've not heard you apologize once for ghosting me!" My tone raises to a pitch that could be described as hysterical, if whoever was describing it were dramatic.

Malcolm opens his mouth, but before he can say anything, the door clinks open, and Vivian steps inside.

"Hello, dear. I'm on my lunch break, and Mum wanted me to see if you had any honey left." She glances from me to Malcolm and back.

"Sure." I smile tightly at her. It takes a monumental effort to look back at Malcolm. "If you want to come back for your health inspection, I'm open during the week from eight in the morning till about four."

"Fine." He turns stiffly to the door. "I'll come back."

As he reaches the door, I call after him. "Oh, and Malcolm? It's just Cordy." I can't help adding under my breath, "Which you should know."

He doesn't even look back at me as he pulls open the door and steps outside. "Good day, Cordelia."

Chapter Twelve
Ronan

"He didn't apologize?"

Cordy's voice sounds tinny across the phone. "No. Not once. He was mad I kept Poppy from him." She sighs. "I suppose I understand, but he was so rude about it."

I press my phone harder against my ear. The service is terrible at Corwynn's place, but I promised Cordy I would try to get him to come around to me, so that's where I am. "When is he coming back? I can be there this time."

"I don't know. He didn't say." She sighs again.

"I'm sorry, Cordy." I want to tell her that her ex sounds like a right piece of work and he shouldn't be allowed near either her or Poppy, but it might not be the right time. Plus, who am I to step between them?

"It was awful. I've never been so mad before in my life. I wanted to slap him. He tried to justify disappearing by basically saying he thought I was a gold-digger. As if his family lawyer wouldn't have made me sign some sort of pre-nup before getting married if that had been the case." Her voice trembles.

"I'm coming over." I can't stand the thought of her crying over some jerk. Except, he's not some jerk. He's the father of Cordy's baby.

"No, it's okay. I'm fine." She sniffs. "You need to help your brother first."

"Corwynn will be fine. You need me right now." Plus, I don't want to tackle my prickly brother and the rat in his bathroom quite yet.

"Ronan, I'm serious. I do want to see you, but you can't leave Corwynn right now."

"He's not even home. He's at the farm," I protest.

"Then go see him on his lunch break. You can come by afterward."

"You promise?" I smile a little. "You drive a hard bargain, Ms. Brown."

She laughs, and I relax. "I promise. I want you to have a happy relationship with your brother. It's important to me, and it's important to you, even if you don't realize it."

"All right. I'll try."

"Thank you. Now go before you've missed his break. I'll see you after."

"Perfect. Maybe you'll even let me kiss you once." I flinch almost as soon as the words are out of my mouth. She doesn't want to kiss me right after she's seen her ex. *I'll try not to dissect that thought too much.*

"Maybe I will." I can hear the smile in her voice, and I feel a warmth spread through me. I'll win her heart after all.

Finding Corwynn is harder than I expect. Then again, I'm not trying very hard. In fact, I'm not trying at all.

Perhaps it is inherently a man's response, but I don't want to talk to my brother about feelings. And I know he doesn't want to either. I don't think I've ever seen Da talk to another man about anything deeper than farming. Da talks to Mam and sometimes to me and Corwynn, but not to others. I know Corwynn is my brother, but there's something strange about us having a heart-to-heart. He's been angry with me for so long that I'm not sure we're capable of having a regular conversation.

All the same, I have to try. Cordy wants me to, and I can't lie to her and tell her I did if I didn't. So I make myself walk into the farmyard where Corwynn works and look around for him. It's not until I run into Mabel, Jack's wife, who points me to the barn that I find him.

He's sitting on an overturned bucket, slowly chewing on a sandwich. I suspect I'm about to ruin his lunch.

"Hey, Cor."

Corwynn jumps and looks up at me. "What are you doing here?"

I look around for another bucket to sit on and spying one behind the door, grab it and bring it over to him. "I know we're not on the best terms . . ." I trail off. That's all I've got.

Corwynn stares at me and stubbornly doesn't say anything. If I didn't like Cordy so much, I'd walk out of this barn this very second. But I've been caught up by her kindness. And beauty. And she sees the best in people. She even overlooks my obvious failings as a brother and encourages me to do better.

Clearing my throat, I try again. "I want us to be brothers. Actual, proper brothers, who share stuff with each other, I guess."

Still, Corwynn doesn't say anything. His half-eaten sandwich dangles from his fingers, and he frowns at me. I search my brain for something else to say. How am I supposed to form a relationship with him if he refuses to talk? No one ever prepared me for this.

With a sigh that actually ruffles my hair and wafts a smell of ham and cheese over me, Corwynn sits up a little straighter. "Fine. What do you want?"

"I said—"

"No, ay, I heard what you said. I'm asking what you really want."

I scowl at him. "I'm trying to be a big brother here. I want you to know I'm here to listen to your side and not just pack you back off to Mam."

Corwynn's eyes narrow. "I don't believe you."

"Well, how do I make you believe me?" I try hard but fail to keep the frustration out of my voice.

Corwynn's eyes flash. "First, you could watch your superior tone with me."

"I don't—"

"Second," he interrupts me firmly, "you can figure it out yourself. I'm not holding your hand so you can step up and care about me."

I sputter. "I do care about you. I've tracked you down to try to make amends—"

He interrupts for a third time, and I can feel my blood boiling. "You only came here because your lady friend wanted you to."

"So what?" I explode. Standing, I glare down at him. "So what if she's the person to push me to be here? I'm here, aren't I? If nothing else, you should be thanking her for making me see some sense." Spinning on my heels, I storm from the barn.

It's not until I reached the road that I realize I may have ruined any chance of reconciling with Corwynn. Shouting at him can't have helped, and I admitted that Cordy was the only reason I was trying in the first place.

Ronan, you big lump.

I'm still fuming when I reach Cordy's shop. I brush open the door and search the store space for her. The jingle of her new bell tinkles over my head.

"Coming." Cordy's voice comes from the kitchen. I make my way to her, sidestepping an abandoned toy car.

"It's me."

"Ronan! That was fast. How'd it go?" Cordy bends over the kitchen table, trying to scoop peas onto a tiny spoon while Poppy watches her brightly.

"It was . . . about as good as your meeting with Malcolm. Well, a bit better, but not by much."

She looks at me over the peas and grimaces. "Well, things can only go up from here, right?"

I can't help but glance at her mouth. *I know one way to make this day better.* Except this is hardly the time to go kissing her. *Get. It. Together. Ronan.*

"Sure." I sit down at her table and make a silly face at a frowning Poppy.

"Oh, don't be so gruff." Cordy attempts to feed the peas to Poppy, who shrieks and jerks her head away. Sighing, Cordy sets the spoon down. "She decided she doesn't like peas anymore. Honestly, I know this is a dumb reason to feel like your life is falling apart . . ." She trails off with a half-laugh.

I reach out and take her hand, smoothing my thumb over the back of her knuckles. "How about you take a break then? Do something that'll get your mind off Malcolm and peas."

She pauses. "Well, I do need to check on my hive with the new queen. I've still been giving them a little bit of sugar water to keep up their spirits, but I should see how they're doing."

"That's my Cordy. Worried about her bugs." I smile at her.

"They're actually not bugs." She perks up in her seat. "They're considered insects but not bugs. Isn't that interesting?"

"It is." Because her face lights up when she talks about bees. I get to my feet. "Well, then. Let's see you in action. Poppy and I will say hi to poor ostracized Go-go, and you can check your hives."

"She's only ostracized because she's a liability to my home and well-being."

I laugh and hold out my arms to Poppy. Not all babies are as friendly as Poppy, but she has warmed to my constant presence in her home and doesn't mind coming to me from time to time. I don't push it though, because I want both her and her mother to be comfortable with me. Poppy looks delighted to be placed in my arms, although I have a sneaking suspicion it's because she's happy to be further from the peas.

The warmth of the late summer sun relaxes me. I don't need to worry about Cordy's ex or my brother right now. I simply need to be present for these two ladies.

I watch Cordy, dressed in her beekeeping gear, go to one of her hives and open the top of it deftly with a small tool. I'm so entirely impressed with her every time I'm around her.

The little backyard that was once a scraggly mess has transformed, with the beehives, the goat pen, and the thriving herb garden. Cordy has made herself a life here. Even if she decides she can't or won't date me, at least she's happy.

Poppy pulls on my beard, and I jolt out of my Cordy-induced reverie.

"Go-go!"

The goat bleats in response and hops her front legs up onto the gate of her enclosure. I playfully tug on one of Poppy's pigtails. "I'm proud of your mam. She's given you a right fine life."

With a mischievous grin, Poppy reaches again for my beard and I gently deflect her. She cackles and then leans toward Go-go, grunting with the effort to close the distance between herself and her pet.

"All right, I get it. I'll remember not to get sappy with you anymore."

Carrying the little girl who is a spitting image of her sweet and funny mam over to the goat pen, something clicks. This is what I want from life. I want goats, bees, and a house that is bound to leak but smells like lavender. Most of all, I want to be a constant presence for these two ladies who already have my heart.

Chapter Thirteen
Ronan

What I don't want is to be in Corwynn's filthy bathroom anymore.

"All right, Cheddar. How do I reach Cor? Why aren't we connecting?" The rat I assume is Cheddar watches me from under the sink. I'm poised to strike, holding a broom and a large pot I found in the hall closet. Corwynn may not mind living with rats, but I'm not about to let this be his life. Even if he hates me.

I sidestep, trying to determine how best to capture Cheddar. I don't want to harm him. I'm simply removing him from the flat. There's a reason humans live inside, and rodents stay outside. The number of plagues started by rats should be a hint to Corwynn, but he's never been big into history. Although if Cheddar comes back, I'm not above sneaking rat poison in. I should have done that to begin with, but Corwynn told me to leave Cheddar alone, and I'm trying not to completely kill our relationship.

Cheddar, the cheeky mite, lunges for the bathroom door. Luckily, I see him coming and with a swift *baf* of my broom, manage to swat him into my pot. Cheddar squeals. I do a quick, dignified jig of victory.

Sensing my distraction, the rat makes a leap for it. With a surprising amount of agility, Cheddar vaults out of the pot and lands with a *slickity-splat* on the bathroom floor.

"You manky thing!"

Cheddar makes a run for it, and this time, he makes it past me and down the hall. I race after him. If I caught him once, I can do it again.

We both round the corner into the kitchen as the front door opens. Corwynn gapes at us from the other side. Spotting an opening to freedom, Cheddar makes a mad dash for the door and sprints past a stunned Corwynn.

"What is going on here?" Corwynn's mouth flaps open as he stares after Cheddar. The rat has made it to the road and is scuttling across the street and into a field.

"I'm sorry, but I can't live with rats, Cor. It's disgusting and weird. If that were a pet rat that you kept up, maybe. But not some street rat."

Corwynn glares at me. "No one is asking you to live here. Go home."

I shake my head. "I can't."

"You can. I don't want you here, so just go."

"Corwynn." I meet his gaze. He starts to scowl at the ground, but I step closer and he glances back up at me. "I'm not going anywhere. I will stay with you until you let me in."

We stare at each other for a moment before Corwynn brushes past me. "I'm knackered. Do whatever you want, but stop chasing animals out of my house."

"Are there more to be chased out?"

But my brother only smirks before going to his room.

Silence hangs for a moment in the tiny flat. I stare mutinously at Corwynn's bedroom door, willing it to open. When nothing happens, I take a deep breath before walking over to lean against the shabby doorframe.

"Can we just talk for a minute?"

I'm answered by silence, so I push on. "I know I haven't been great at all this . . . talking stuff, but I'm trying to figure out what you want."

More silence. *All right, if he wants to be this way, he can have his rats and I'll leave.*

Even as the thought has me turning to go, I stop myself. What did Cordy say? Something about how I need to be better at listening. Except I don't know how to do that when he won't talk to me.

"Hey," I call suddenly through the door as a thought hits me. "Do you remember when you were four or maybe five and Da took ill? Mam had to run to town to get him some medicine and she left me in charge. Do you remember that you wanted so badly to help Da that you took it into your head to make him bacon and toast? I found you in the kitchen, lying on the floor where you'd dropped the frying pan. It landed partially on your arm, and you were screaming something fierce."

I clear my throat at the memory. "I was so scared. Not because I thought Mam would kill me for not having kept a better eye on you, but because you're my little brother and I love you. I've never driven faster than when I drove you to the hospital that day."

Finally, Corwynn's quiet voice floats through the door. "Why're you telling me this?"

"Because I love you. Because I've been a git. Because I'm supposed to protect you and I keep failing to do that and I'm sorry." The last bit rushes out of me.

Something moves behind Corwynn's door. It cracks open just enough for me to see my little brother's face. He raises an eyebrow at me. "You've done a fine job protecting me from Cheddar."

"And you still haven't thanked me for that," I quip back.

He smirks and edges the door closed. Before it snaps shut, he adds, "I really am knackered."

I take the hint and step back. "All right, I'll just be going. I love you," I add as an afterthought.

"Yeah, yeah. Don't go soft on me then, ay?"

I can't stop the grin that spread across my face. I'd call this a successful conversation. I can't wait to tell Cordy.

What I hope to find is Cordy alone when I get to her shop. It feels like ages since I last had some one-on-one time with her. Since she checked her hive earlier this week, I've been doubling down on trying to talk to Corwynn, and she's been busy getting her honey ready to sell.

But when I push open her door, I see she isn't alone. A blond man is scowling around the room as if it just insulted his mother. Standing in the doorway to the kitchen, Cordy watches him with an equally stormy expression.

"Hey," I say, not wanting to interrupt whatever is happening but also wanting to make Cordy smile.

And she does. I'm relieved when her features slide into that beautiful smile of hers.

"Ronan."

I'm not exactly sure when I fell in love with Cordy Brown. I'm fairly certain by how she sighs my name that the feeling is mutual.

"Do you need anything?" I cross the room and bend to kiss her cheek.

"Ah, no." She glances at the man and then looks back at me and lowers her voice. "That's the health inspector."

Ah. I straighten and smile at the man who glares back. Out of the side of my mouth, I whisper to Cordy, "Sour-looking bloke."

"Yeah, he's also Malcolm."

Wait, what? I pin my full attention on her. "Malcolm-your-ex Malcolm? Why didn't you say he's also the health inspector?" It takes momentous efforts to keep my voice at a whisper.

"I didn't think about it," she hisses back. "I was caught up in telling you about his excuses."

"And who are you?"

I turn and find Malcolm standing right next to me. Up close, he's even more of a pale fish, although he's handsome in an "I stepped out of a uni catalog" kind of way. I can see him wearing a sweater tied around his neck while playing tennis. Miserable pox.

"I'm Ronan," I state simply. No need to give him more than that.

Malcolm's scowl deepens, and he wheels on Cordy. "Is this why you're so upset with me? You've got a boyfriend who's filling your head with—"

Cordy flares up. "First, he's not my boyfriend yet. Second, if he was, it wouldn't matter to you anyway."

I can't help but bask in her use of *yet*. Malcolm notices my basking though, and zeros in on me.

"What are you smirking at, you git?"

"Malcolm," Cordy snaps.

"Cordelia." He turns to her beseechingly. "We loved each other once. We even have a beautiful daughter—"

"Do not bring Poppy into this." There's a warning in Cordy's voice that if I were Malcolm, would make me back off, but the man continues on, unfazed.

"I don't see why we can't get back together."

Cordy levels a glare at him. "Because I know the truth."

This makes both Malcolm and me pause. I feel like I'm a spectator at an intense game of tennis.

"Know what?" But I can tell from Malcolm's face that he has an idea of what Cordy knows.

"I talked to my mother, Malcolm. It's over. I know."

Okay. What is happening?

"What do you know?" I ignore Malcolm's hateful glare and take Cordy's hand. "What's going on?"

I notice then that her shoulders are trembling. She looks at me with large eyes and blows out a sigh. "I talked to Mom this morning. Apparently, Malcolm called her at some point while I was pregnant with Poppy and asked if I was telling the truth about having a baby. She told him yes, but . . . then he never reached out to me. He knew the whole time."

I barely have enough time to comprehend her words when Malcolm nearly shouts, "I didn't know what to do!"

"Don't you dare wake up Poppy," Cordy snarls at him.

Mercifully, Malcolm lowers his voice. "I didn't want to end up in a loveless relationship over some—" He stops dead. But the damage is done.

I see Cordy's face contort in anger and hurt, but even I know it's not hurt for herself. She's hurt for her little girl.

Something inside of me snaps. It's one thing to be a major jerk. I can almost understand why he pretended he didn't know—almost—but for Malcolm to refer to a child, especially his own child, in such a callous way, has me nearly as furious as Cordy.

Crash.

Cordy gasps as Malcolm lands on the ground, knocking into the same honey table that Go-go wrecked. It takes me a full second to realize I've hit him. My fist is still out, my arm trembling from the effort of not hitting him a second time.

"Bloody—" Malcolm's nose is bleeding profusely, and he stumbles up to his feet, his eyes blazing in fury. With a wild swing that reminds me of my uncle Marv after a second glass of wine, he comes at me.

Distantly, I hear Cordy yelp, but all my concentration is now on getting Malcolm out of Cordy's shop before he breaks something else. He's already broken her heart twice. The least I can do is keep him from breaking her livelihood as well.

Grabbing Malcolm's shirt with both fists, I heave him out the door. With a frantic jingle, the door swings closed behind me, and I throw Malcolm on the scruffy grass. He lands with a grunt on his hands and knees. I stifle the urge to kick him. *I need to get my anger under control.*

With a disgruntled yell, Malcolm launches himself up. He's beet red, and he roars as he comes at me. I catch his right hook easily and pull him closer to keep him from swinging at me again. The technique works, and Malcolm flounders in confusion. I shove him, and he falls again into the grass. Dull green stains the knees of his pants, and when Malcolm catches sight of it, his red face grows even darker.

"These pants are brand new," he sputters, staring at the grass stains.

I can't believe what I'm hearing. "You come into Cordy's life, lie to her face about not knowing you have a daughter, and you're worried about grass stains on your pants?"

"I haven't done anything wrong," Malcolm spits.

"Leave, Malcolm," I say through clenched teeth. For a split second, it looks as if Malcolm may argue, but he takes in my anger and decides against whatever he was thinking of saying. Slowly, he gets to his feet, and after one last baleful glare, he turns and walks back to his sleek company car.

Turning around, I find Cordy standing in the doorway. She's blinking hard and staring at Malcolm's back with a mix of emotions. Does it make me a jerk that I'm slightly relieved she looks anything but pleased?

"Hey." I keep my voice gentle. "He's a major tool. Don't let him get to you."

"You heard what he said. Loveless relationship. I mean, I don't want to get back together, but he's acting as if our time together at college was a joke. And I'm not sure what he was going to say about Poppy, but he wasn't even referring to her as a human." Her rapid blinking won't stop the tears now. I step forward to shield her from seeing Malcolm drive away and pull her into a hug. She crumples against me, her face buried in my chest as she cries.

"Shhh," I whisper, wishing I had something else to say.

"He knew, Ronan."

I squeeze her tighter. "I know, love."

"He knew this whole time—" She breaks off in a sob.

"He doesn't deserve you or her," I murmur.

She leans back and wipes under her eyes. "I don't even know why I'm crying. I got over him being a jerk a year ago. I thought I was done with all that . . . with him."

"You're crying because your daughter's father was rude to you and her."

She glances up at me and somewhere in the back of my mind, I note that even while crying, she's beautiful. She sniffs sharply and wipes at her nose with the back of her sleeve, and I can't help a tiny smile.

"When did you get so wise when it comes to family matters?"

"Oh, haha. I'll have you know, I chased a rat out of my brother's flat earlier, and he didn't even threaten to kick me out." She looks completely confused. All I can think to do is to hug her again. "Never mind. You're allowed to be upset."

Against my shoulder, she whispers, "I might be upset for a while."

"You're allowed to be," I say again and squeeze her tighter. *If Malcolm shows his face around here again* . . . I cut my thoughts short. I'm not opposed to fighting for Cordy's hand, but I'm not exactly sure if she wants me to or not.

Cordy leans back to look at me. Then she tips up onto her toes and kisses me lightly on the cheek. "Thank you."

Okay. I would fight a bear for this woman.

Chapter Fourteen
Cordy

I try really hard not to be bitter. I've spent the last few days blasting my favorite music and making myself entirely too many cups of coffee. I've even tried planning out next month's agenda for the store. But my brain keeps circling back to Malcolm. And because I'm trying really hard not to hate my daughter's father, I finally decide I need a distraction.

"Hey Pops, do you want to go for a walk?" I'm already packing up her stroller. Poppy has been up for the past hour, playing with Go-go on the kitchen floor.

Okay, so letting my goat into the house may or may not have been a small act of revenge on Malcolm. But I've kept the baby gate in the kitchen doorway ever since Poppy's birthday, ensuring that neither my toddler nor my goat can get into the store. Ruining my business isn't on my agenda; just knowing how infuriated Malcolm would be if he could see my kitchen is enough.

"We're not being bitter, remember?" I mumble to myself as I strap Poppy into her stroller and hand her a sippy cup.

"Go-go come?" Poppy bubbles cheerfully.

"Sure, we can bring Go-go." I squat down to secure the goat's collar and leash.

"Yeah!" Poppy shouts and waves her sippy cup triumphantly.

I can't help but laugh at her enthusiasm, but at the same time, burning anger toward Malcolm surges up again. He actually pretended to not know about this amazing little girl and then had the nerve to try to guilt me for not telling him? At least Mom told me the truth.

Honestly, I'd avoided calling Mom to tell her about Malcolm being back for as long as I could. I didn't want her to immediately tell me to come back home, and I didn't want her stressing about his rude behavior. When we did speak, I could tell that it was killing her to tell me Malcolm had known.

When I demanded to know why she hadn't told me when Malcolm called her, she said she was trying to give him time to reach out to me. "Then by the time I realized he wasn't going to reach out, I thought telling you would only hurt you all over again."

"But I thought he already knew," I huffed. "I didn't know he thought I was lying."

After a tiny pause, Mom whispered, "Oh, yeah," before apologizing. And here we are. All of us fully understand Malcolm is a lying jerk and he's always been a lying jerk.

"Boy, I really know how to pick 'em," I grumble as I push Poppy's stroller up the sidewalk.

I now realize where my feet have taken me. Completely on autopilot, I've ended up at the end of Barney's driveway. I can see Barney's knobby knit hat bobbing around his overgrown garden, and I push my way over to where he can see us.

"Ah, my two favorite girls." Barney beams at us. "Come in for a cup of tea."

By the time the tea has been made and poured into cups, Barney has heard the whole sorry tale of Malcolm and his betrayal. He's also had a blushing recounting of how Ronan is basically my knight in shining armor.

"And what do you plan to do about this whole Malcolm business?" Barney settles himself into his little armchair and watches Poppy feed Go-go biscuits.

"I . . . I don't know. Can I report him to the institute of horrible men?" I try to smile through my weak joke, but Barney just gazes steadily at me. I sigh. "What can I do, Barney? I can't let him back into my life. Or Poppy's life."

"No one is saying you should, lass." Barney's spoon clinks sharply on his teacup. He stares into his tea for a moment before looking up. "You can work on forgiving him first before deciding what else to do."

"I don't know if I can ever let him be around me or Poppy," I say quietly. "He *lied* for over a year about not knowing about Pops."

"Forgiving him doesn't mean you drop all your boundaries. Just because you forgive someone, doesn't mean you let them back to do the same thing they did before." Barney smiles reassuringly. "Forgiving Malcolm is more for you than it is for him. Your heart will never fully heal if you don't."

"I don't even know where to start," I say, a little petulantly. I'll be honest. Forgiving Malcolm sounds insanely hard, and I kind of don't want to. Not that I'll tell Barney that.

Barney mulls this over for a moment. "Perhaps you'd like to come to church with me this Sunday."

I blink in surprise. For a moment I wonder what that has to do with my problem, but then I realize what he means. "I don't think church is going to make me more forgiving."

Barney continues to watch me over his glasses. "Have you ever been to church?"

"Well, no, not since I was very little. But Barney, I wouldn't fit in at church. It's not that I'm opposed," I add with a shrug. "But church people don't usually care for . . . my type."

"What type is that?" Barney looks genuinely confused.

"Single mothers," I say with another shrug. I have a vivid image of my aunt Mel calling me to ask when my wedding was after I told Mom about my positive test. It's not just Mel though; I've seen how people like Sydney Waterford from the employment office react when they find out I'm single and a mom. You'd think it wouldn't be such a big deal anymore, but here I am.

Barney still looks confused. "Why would that matter?"

"Barney . . . come on. People look down on single moms all the time. It's not exactly in line with Christian teaching." I smile to show I'm not hurt by this.

With a sharp shake of his white head, Barney leans forward in his seat. "My dear, it's true marriage is highly encouraged, and I would warrant it's to try to lessen the amount of Malcolms in the world, but that doesn't mean you aren't welcome. As for Poppy, all babies are gifts and bring joy. She is a blessing, and while you and Malcolm weren't and aren't a good match, God saw to it that Poppy would be here. She is not here by mistake, and neither are you. The doors are always open to you both, and if anyone tells you otherwise, send them straight to me."

He looks so fierce that I laugh a little. "I appreciate that, Barney. Really, I do."

"Why hasn't anyone told you that before?" Barney seems affronted by the lack of charity shown by his fellow believers.

Shaking my head, I reach out to catch Poppy as she barrels toward me. Cuddling her into my lap, I focus on her and Go-go. "No one has said we were not welcome exactly, but I didn't want to put Poppy into a situation where someone could be ugly to her."

"I understand that." The wrinkles around Barney's eyes crinkle as he smiles. "But Cordy, people shouldn't keep you away from God. People may be rude from time to time, and there are some in the church who can be unkind, but those people do not represent Christ. If you don't wish to come to church with me, you do not have to. I am merely saying that people who may or may not say something to you shouldn't be your reason to stay away. Especially if you think you could gain healing by going."

His words hang in the air between us. I'm not sure what to say. I haven't thought about God since Aunt Mel called. I couldn't change my situation. I wasn't about to force Malcolm to marry me, so what else could I do but ignore people like Mel?

Barney leans forward. "I don't want to overwhelm you. It always pains me to see when those who would call themselves followers of Christ actively make others feel unwelcome."

Looking into Barney's eyes, so magnified by his glasses, I can see he's genuine. "I can't promise to come with you, but I appreciate that you want to make up for other people's rudeness. It's not something you have to do, though."

He opens his mouth to protest, but I lean forward and pat his hand. "Thank you for trying, though. And thank you for listening to me. You've done a lot for me since I moved here."

He smiles. "You remind me a little of my daughter. Jack's sister moved to America when she was about your age, and I always prayed someone would help her. I told myself if anyone needed my help when they moved here to Arbury, I'd be that person for them."

Okay, Cordy. Don't cry.

I clear my throat. "That's incredibly sweet of you."

"Ah, well . . ." Barney turns gruff, apparently catching sight of my watery eyes. "Anyway, the offer always stands."

"Thank you," I whisper.

"Now then. More tea?" Barney gets to his feet, but I wave him off.

"No, no, it's okay. I've got to get back home. I'm nearly out of honey again, and I'm going to take a crack at harvesting some more this afternoon. I think it'll be the last time I can this summer."

Gathering up Poppy and Go-go only takes a few minutes, even with Go-go trying to hide under Barney's armchair. Barney stands at the door and waves at us as we head down the road. I get all the way to the bend in the road before I start to cry. Not just because Barney is being the grandfather I've always wanted, and not even because Malcolm is the baby daddy I never wanted. It's everything. Barney, Malcolm, my business being threatened, Poppy getting bigger, time moving too quickly, and Ronan.

The tears regarding Ronan are happy tears though. Maybe a little sad because we haven't had a date yet, but mostly happy.

By the time I reach the main road in Arbury, the tears have dried. I have a feeling that running into Vivian with tears dripping down my face wouldn't be great. She'd want to usher me into her café and bring cup after cup of coffee, which would be sweet of her and would be normally appreciated, but I want to be alone right now. As alone as I can be with a one-year-old and a goat.

My shoulders relax as we turn into our driveway. Go-go jumps forward, and Poppy squeals. The rest of the tension fades, and I laugh too. I love that Poppy loves our home. She's a much better person than I am, full of joy and not bogged down by little bits of nothing.

That's it. I resolve to be more like my daughter and try harder to be joyful. And my resolve makes it all the way to my front door before crumbling. Pinned to the wood is a note in familiar handwriting.

Consider this your informal warning, Cordelia, and find a job.

Only one person calls me Cordelia, and only one person has the power to kill the job I currently have.

"Malcolm." His name feels like a rock coming out of my mouth. The edges of my vision go a little blurry. Who the heck does he think he is?

I jam the door open and march us inside. Unhooking Go-go, I shoo her into the kitchen before releasing Poppy from the stroller. I so badly want to scream, but I can't let Poppy see me freak out. Pulling out my phone, I check the time. It's unfortunately not nap time. I resolve to stew in silence while trying not to let my negative thoughts fill the room.

What do I do now? What in the world am I supposed to do? I have a flashback to Barney telling me to forgive Malcolm, but that leaves a horrible taste in my mouth. I don't exactly know how to forgive someone *and* set firm boundaries.

Who am I kidding? I don't want to forgive Malcolm. I want to hate him and . . . and throw eggs at him or something.

I watch Poppy work on a small wooden puzzle, slamming the farm animals into random holes. Suddenly, the overwhelming urge to call Mom hits me. Which is crazy, because I can honestly say that since moving here, I've been a little apprehensive about talking to Mom, and yet, I need to talk to her.

I dial her number. Three rings later, she picks up.

"Cordy? Is Poppy okay? What happened?" I can hear the panic in her voice, and I feel guilty. I hardly ever call Mom without a scheduled reason.

"Mom, she's fine. No one is hurt."

"Oh, thank God," Mom gasps.

I fight the urge to roll my eyes. *Chill, Cordy, she's just happy no one is hurt.*

"No, it's Malcolm again." And I tell her. Actually, I rant at her. Before I know it, I'm bringing up moments from our relationship from two years ago and tying it to his current betrayal. I *knew* that his not liking french fries was a sign.

Maybe that's not fair, to bring up his past.

Maybe it is. I mean, he was a liar back then, and he's still a liar now.

A little hand pats my leg, and I look down to see Poppy grinning up at me, completely unaware of the tears I keep swiping away.

"Mama, look!" "Look" comes out sounding more like "loo," but she helpfully points while speaking.

I turn to see she's gotten a hold of a pen and has cheerfully made art on my kitchen wall. Staring at the blue lines on my recently scrubbed wall, a well of hysteria bubbles up in my chest.

I burst out laughing. Not my best choice of reaction, because Poppy immediately looks so pleased with herself that I know she's going to have a hard time understanding why she can't draw on the walls again.

"Cordy?" Mom asks.

"Poppy drew on the wall," I say through giggles.

"Don't encourage her," Mom yelps in my ear. "She'll think she should do it again to make you laugh."

"I know, Mom," I say, still laughing. "It's just . . . after everything else . . ."

There's a tiny silence as I gather up the pen and make sure Poppy doesn't have anything else that could give me more cleaning to do. I keep the phone pressed to my ear, waiting for Mom to drop some wisdom into my lap. I'm impressed with her for not telling me to move home yet. That's usually her go-to solution. Just come back to the States.

"Cordy." Mom's voice makes me automatically tense up. "I'm really sorry, hon. I wish this would have gone differently. Remember the first time I met Malcolm?"

I pause, thinking back. I remember setting up a time for them to meet over video chat. Between mine, Malcolm's, and Mom's schedules, it had been a nightmare, but we'd eventually found a time to chat. And then Malcolm canceled at the last minute.

"I don't think I remember you ever meeting him." I'm ninety percent sure we never rescheduled that chat.

"I didn't," Mom says flatly. "That's my point. You two dated for a year, and not once did I get to talk to him. I saw his picture, and you told me about him all the time, but I never spoke a word to that boy."

"Oh." I draw up short. "Never? Not even over the phone?"

"He was always on his way out the door when I called," Mom huffs. "Or he had a very important phone call to make."

I flinch at her tone. Not because I'm offended by her, but because I can now kind of see why she never seemed very excited about Malcolm when I brought him up. No wonder she wanted me to move back home when I told her I was pregnant and that Malcolm disappeared.

"I'm sorry, Mom. I didn't realize."

She sighs hard into my ear. "Oh, honey. I didn't want you pining after some man-child who couldn't even meet your mom." Then a dam breaks, and I can hear her voice become more choked as she talks faster. "When you said you were going to stay in London, after everything that had happened, I was so scared you were staying for *him*. You deserve so much better than that . . . than Malcolm Carmichael the Second. You should be with someone who is there for you no matter what, and who is there when times are hard. Falling in love is easy, but sometimes you have to choose to love someone. Not all the time, because if you have to choose all the time that's forcing it, but in the hard moments. In the 'we have no money' moments or the 'someone is trying to pull us apart' moments, that's when you choose to love, and Malcolm didn't." She breathes hard. "And of course, I wanted to be near Poppy, and I would love to see her grow up, but . . . well, it was mostly that Malcolm hurt you so much. I'm sorry, Cordy. I wish I could have done something."

My eyes have decided to stop listening to my brain and are now producing an insane amount of tears. "Mom, I didn't stay for him. I stayed because I've been in love with this country for as long as I can remember. I stayed for me."

"That's all I needed to hear," Mom whispers. I can hear her sniff, and I wish I could throw my arms around her. All this time I wasted, thinking she didn't care about my happiness when she only wanted me to be happy and in a healthy relationship. "I still miss my grandchild though," she adds, and I laugh.

"I know you do."

"Maybe I need to plan a visit and come see what this amazing England is all about."

Something weird is happening in my chest. It's as if I've been holding my breath for the past five years, ever since I boarded my plane to attend King's College, and now I can let it go. I can feel my body physically relaxing, and I clear my throat to chase away the second batch of tears that threaten.

"Really? You want to visit?"

"Yes." Mom sounds just as emotional as me. *So that's who I get it from.* "I want to see your life. Your real life. I promise not to be a Debbie Downer about it either."

"I'd love that."

"Okay. Well, I'll plan a trip then." She even sounds excited about it.

Maybe something good has come from Malcolm's crash landing into my life.

No, I'm not going to give him credit for Mom and me taking a step closer to each other. Moving to this tiny, nowhere town was the best thing that ever happened to me. Arbury holds so many people that have somehow made my life better.

Chapter Fifteen
Cordy

"There's no real reason why Malcolm can shut me down, right?" I lift my head from my arms and look hopefully at Vivian.

Paperwork, pictures of my shop, cups of coffee, and muffin crumbs are strewn across my kitchen table. It's late in the evening, Poppy's already in bed, and Vivian is helping me build a case to keep my shop. She's the only person I know who runs her own business, and the truth is, Vivian has been one of my biggest supporters since I moved in.

"Well, Go-go has a proper enclosure, and if he brings up what Harold Smith saw, we can say that not only was the store closed, but someone other than yourself was holding Go-go at the time." Vivian fluffs a stack of papers and taps them against the table.

"What, do you mean Ronan? I'm not going to blame Ronan for having Go-go in the shop." I frown at her over my own stack of papers.

Vivian shrugs. "I doubt he'd mind, especially if it allowed you to keep your shop."

"Viv, I can't blame Ronan. I let Go-go into my house in the first place. Remember how much she scared your mom the first time she came by? Go-go has been in the shop before, because I let her."

"I'm just saying he'd be your scapegoat." Vivian chuckles at her joke.

I give her a mock eye roll and smile a little. "Well, I'm not going to ask him to do that."

"What was Malcolm's other reason for shutting you down?"

"Besides personal revenge?" I sigh and pick up a picture of the shop I'd snapped earlier. Peering at the picture, I try to see anything that could get me shut down. Earlier, Vivian and I both inspected the shop twice before deciding we were going to go cross-eyed, and Vivian took a few pictures.

"That's not a legal reason," Vivian says tartly.

"Yeah, well, I don't think Malcolm cares about legality right now. This is all personal revenge."

Vivian holds out her cup of coffee in a salute. "Malcolm is a complete maggot."

"That he is," says a deep, musical voice.

I look up to see Ronan in the kitchen doorway. "Your door was open, Cordy. You need to keep it locked."

"Yeah, so I can keep ruffians like you out," I tease.

He shoots me a little wink and comes to sit next to me. "I wanted to see what my favorite lady is up to."

"Oh, nothing. Just trying to save my livelihood, as you do."

He wraps an arm around my shoulders, not fooled by my chipper tone. For a second, we both stare down at the table. Sighing, I lean into Ronan. "What am I going to do, guys? Do I move back to South Carolina? And then what? Use my infinite expertise in beekeeping and classic literature?"

Ronan places a quick kiss on the top of my head. "Hey, shh, you don't have to move, love."

"Can we get Malcolm fired or moved off your case?" Vivian glances up from a stack of receipts. "You've been doing everything by the book, and you've kept great records. Maybe we could call his superiors and tell them that Malcolm is harassing you." She looks fiercely between our faces. "Because that's what he's doing. He's harassing you."

"Is he?" I raise an eyebrow at her. "I mean, 'harassment' is a pretty strong word."

"He's threatening to shut you down because he's mad at you." Vivian's voice tops normal speaking volume, and I make a shushing motion to quiet her down. "Sorry. But really, you can't be making excuses for him. He lies about knowing about Poppy, and then when you call him out on it, he tries to shut down the very thing that is putting food into your daughter's mouth. He's taking food away from Poppy."

"Vivian—"

"Cordy, what he's doing is awful, and he should get fired for that," Vivian says firmly.

I sigh. "Look, I'm trying not to hate him. In fact, I'm trying to forgive him so that I *don't* hate him."

Vivian gapes at me. "Forgive him?"

"Oh, don't look at me like that. I'm not forgiving him for him. I'm forgiving him for me."

"What are you talking about?"

I sit up without dislodging Ronan's arm. "I was talking to Barney, and he told me I should try to forgive Malcolm for me. I don't have to let him come stomping through my life and I should set boundaries, but for my own happiness, I'm going to try to forgive him."

Ronan gives me a little squeeze. "How are you going to do that?"

"I don't know," I admit. "But I think it starts with me not hating him." I give Vivian a meaningful look.

She frowns but then shrugs. "Whatever you think."

"I don't think it's a bad idea to get him transferred off my case, though," I add.

"I'll call around in the morning then." Vivian stands briskly. "And I'll come by once I have news. You two have a good night." She packs her handbag with the few extra photos and gives us both a smile. "We'll get through this."

I smile back at her. "Thanks, Vivian."

"I'll show myself out." She shoots Ronan a wink before hurrying out of the kitchen.

"Finally." Ronan grins as he shifts me to face him. "I've been waiting to have some alone time with you."

I attempt to be coy and peer up at him through my lashes. Except I don't think I'm doing it right, and I change tactics to look down at my hands in my lap. "I've been thinking about our date."

"Shall we set a time for one finally? We've been talking about it for months now."

I swat his arm. "It's only been a few weeks."

"It feels like I've been waiting for this date for years, my dear." He grins, and I take a moment to admire his face. It still surprises me that I'm into his beard. I've never been into the rugged look before. I have a weird urge to tug on his beard, and instead, I fiddle with the hem of my shirt to keep my hands occupied.

"I very much want to kiss you." Ronan's gaze is on my mouth, and I fight every temptation to pull him close to me.

"I know," I whisper. Okay, I may be staring at his mouth too.

"What am I waiting for?" I'm not sure if he's asking me or himself.

There's a tiny pause. I bite my lower lip. "I don't know."

I see the shift in his eyes, and I know that he understands. His fingers gently caress my jawline, tipping my face upward. His eyes darken, and I sink into their depths. I never truly appreciated brown eyes before. Ronan's eyes are almost amber, a few shades deeper than my honey.

And then his mouth is on mine, and the warmth I saw in his eyes spreads through my body. My stomach gives a flip, and a weird, tingly feeling sweeps up my fingers and toes. He smells a little bit like leather, and I commit that to memory.

Oh. My. Gosh.

With a soft sigh, Ronan murmurs, "Cordy—"

"Shhh." I reach up and pull him in for one more kiss. You know, to test if I feel the same thing. Which I do.

This man might turn me into an addict if his kisses do that to me each time. It would probably be better if I took a break from kissing him, right?

I feel Ronan's hand in my hair, keeping me pressed close, and I immediately tell my inner voice to shush. I'm not about to make him stop. In fact, I think I'll take up residence here on his mouth.

But of course, we have to stop. Because we're trying to take it slow, and technically, I am in the middle of saving my shop.

Well. Maybe just one more.

Chapter Sixteen
Cordy

The high of Ronan's kisses is still going strong the next morning. That is, until a knock on my door reminds me of my current problem. My blond problem, who apparently wants to ruin my life. And his daughter's life.

"Already?" I groan. Poppy looks up from her Cheerios, and I drop a kiss on her forehead. "I love you, Pops." She grins up at me and holds out a handful of soggy cereal.

I would never have thought soggy cereal was something I would take from someone, but all it takes is twenty pounds of cuteness and I'm peeling wet oats into my hands. And promptly throwing them away, because *ew*.

Another knock.

"I'm coming," I call. "Impatient jerk," I add in an undertone.

Before I open the door, I take a second to breathe. I don't need to come across as aggressive. It'll make things worse, and Malcolm has enough aggression for both of us. Pulling open the door, I try to keep my face calm.

Except I'm not staring at Malcolm's pug nose. Instead, I'm looking at a middle-aged woman with angular features and tight lips.

"Oh, hello." I smile widely at her. "The store is open if you'd like to come in."

"Are you Cordelia Brown?" The woman has a clipped accent that makes her sound like a queen. This is someone who isn't accustomed to being denied things.

"Ah, yes, I'm Cordy." I shift nervously on the doorstep. Is this Malcolm's supervisor?

The woman tips her immaculately styled blonde head toward me, as if she's taking me in. Well, she's getting a somewhat messy introduction. I'm wearing comfy jeans and an oversized sweater covered in the oatmeal that was my first attempt at Poppy's breakfast. At least Go-go is in her pen and not here.

"I'd like to speak to you about Malcolm Carmichael."

Oh, for crying out loud. I knew it. All I can do now is hope that she's here to apologize for her employee's actions and assure me I'm not getting shut down.

I take a step back and gesture for her to come inside. "Would you like some coffee?"

Closing the door behind her, I usher my visitor into the kitchen. Poppy looks up from her breakfast and opens her mouth to let a bit of cereal dribble out. I wipe her mouth and tut at her. I'm so glad she woke up in a good mood this morning. Lately, she's been giving me sunny dispositions, and it's one of my favorite stages.

"Oh, hello there." The lady's clipped accent softens when she spots Poppy.

"This is my daughter, Poppy," I say over my shoulder as I grab another coffee mug from my cabinet.

"It's an absolute pleasure, Poppy." The woman circles the table to sit nearer to my beaming child. She's cooing at Poppy, her eyes wide, as if she's never seen a baby before.

A horrible thought strikes me. What if this woman is some sort of baby kidnapper? I didn't even ask to see credentials before I let her waltz into my home. *Okay, Cordy, don't go ballistic. Ask to see some ID.*

"I'm sorry, I didn't get your name." I'm pretty proud of how steady my voice is.

"Oh." She looks up from Poppy. "Yes, I'm sorry. I'm Charlotte. Charlotte Carmichael. I'm Poppy's grandmother."

Has the whole world gone crazy? Am *I* crazy? How is it possible that for nearly two years I haven't heard from a single Carmichael, and now two of them have shown up on my doorstep within a few days of each other? Not a bit of interest in me or Poppy, and now I have a doting grandma sitting in my kitchen sipping coffee and using her Coco Chanel scarf to play peek-a-boo with my daughter.

"So you're telling me you had no idea you had a granddaughter." I eye Charlotte with suspicion. She apologized for not reaching out sooner, but only elaborated enough to say she hadn't known.

"I did not." Charlotte shakes her head. "I do remember Malcolm dating an American girl while at uni, but we never met. One day he came home to say that he and the girl—you, I suppose—were no longer together. I asked him why, and he only said he thought you were after his money."

I immediately bristle, but Charlotte holds up one of her perfectly manicured hands. "I believed him, because he had a few past girlfriends who had shown interest only in his money. I had no way of knowing the whole story, and Malcolm's never been one to share his dating life with me."

"But now he's told you?" I need all the clarification I can get. It makes sense, I guess. He's been caught in a lie and can't deny our existence anymore.

"Not quite." Charlotte's lips quirk in an apologetic smile. "I received a call from a lovely American named Heather Brown last night."

"Mom?" I gape at her.

"Yes, it appears she tracked me down via social media. When she told me I had a granddaughter, I nearly hung up on her. I'll admit I thought she was trying to gain money for her grandchild. She asked if my son had ever dated an American girl named Cordelia, and I realized she might be telling the truth. Afterward, she sent me a picture of Poppy, and I could see the family resemblance."

We both look at Poppy. I try to remember if I saw much of Malcolm in Poppy, but it seems like decades ago that I saw them side-by-side. She has the same eye shape as me, and her chin is rounded like mine. Even her ears look like mine.

"She favors you a great deal," Charlotte says, like she can read my mind. "But I do see Malcolm in her expressions. Especially when she smiles."

I fight the urge to argue with her. How is it fair that Poppy has Malcolm's smile when he wants to take that smile away? *Okay, Cordy. Calm it down.*

Taking a deep breath, I exhale slowly. I can't be jealous of Poppy's DNA. That's not going to help anything. It's starting to make sense that Barney said I need to forgive Malcolm for my own sake.

This is the kind of moment in which I wish I liked the taste of wine, because I could really use a little sip of something to get me to calm down. Then again, I shouldn't be drinking to cope with emotions. Frustration wells inside of me, and I need to do something about it. I smack my hands down on the table.

Charlotte and Poppy both jump. "Sorry." I smile weakly at Charlotte. "I feel like I'm having a midlife crisis. Two Carmichaels in one week, and Malcolm wants to shut me down . . ." I trail off. I'm not exactly sure what Charlotte knows, and I have even less of an idea if she's on my side. For all I know, she wants to get custody of Poppy.

"Ah, yes. About that." Charlotte frowns and absentmindedly hands her scarf to Poppy. I open my mouth to warn her against handing her five-hundred-dollar scarf to a baby, but she waves a hand. "Don't worry, love, it's last season's. Anyway, about my son threatening to shut you down. There is no need to worry about that."

"But I kind of think there is." I fold my arms across my middle. "I don't know what he has for a reason exactly, but I'm sure he could do it."

Charlotte shakes her head. "No, dear, you misunderstand. He will not shut down the business of my grandchild's mother. I won't have Poppy or you out on the streets."

"I do own the house," I say reassuringly. "We wouldn't be homeless."

One of Charlotte's perfect eyebrows arch. "That is beside the point, dear. You have nothing to worry about, and we'll leave it at that." She turns back to Poppy and reaches out to tickle her. Poppy shrieks with glee. "She truly is a precious little girl. I wondered this on the drive over. Has she been baptized?"

A dawning realization hits me. Slowly, I take a seat at the table across from her. "Mrs. Carmichael—"

"Call me Charlotte, please."

"Charlotte. I'm not going to marry Malcolm."

She looks at me as if I've proclaimed I won't marry the Queen. "I didn't suppose you'd want to after how he behaved himself. What does that have to do with anything?"

"Well, you asked if Poppy has been baptized, and I didn't want you to think I would get married to Malcolm just because he's her father." Charlotte still looks nonplussed. "I have an aunt who is religious, and . . ." I wave my hands, hoping to indicate that marriage to Malcolm is somehow tied to her baptism question.

"Oh, dear." Charlotte shakes her head. "I asked because I adore seeing baptism pictures. Little babies in white, frilly outfits are always precious. I have several watercolor paintings in my dining room that picture baptisms. And I have many special memories from Malcolm's christening. This has nothing to do with marrying my son. There are many good and godly reasons for marriage. I'll admit that in a perfect world, I'd love to see you and Malcolm together, but it is not a perfect world, and my son has not been a good man. He has broken your trust and abandoned you and his daughter. If he were to have changed in the past year, I would encourage you both to get to know each other again, but the truth is, I see no change in him. Now, if he were to make an effort, I would hope you would listen to him, but I'm under no delusions that you two would get back together."

I stare at her. I don't have any words. She admits that Malcolm wasn't a good man?

"I don't want to push you further from him, for Poppy's sake." Charlotte seems to have read my mind. "Try not to hate him."

I take in her serious, yet sad expression. There is something in her eyes that breaks my heart a little. What if one day I have to tell someone that Poppy hasn't been a good person? That would kill a little part of me.

Reaching out, I take her hand. "I'm sorry, Charlotte. I don't want to keep him from Poppy. I don't want to hate him either." I pause to think about it. "I don't think I hate him."

She leans toward Poppy and snags the corner of her scarf to wipe her eyes. Poppy allows the scarf to be tugged out of her mouth a little where she was gnawing on it. Charlotte sniffs and pushes the scarf back to Poppy.

"I will speak to him about this whole mess. I'll encourage him to think of his daughter and less of himself. He could use someone to remind him that his actions affect others. I do hope I can see Poppy from time to time?" She blinks at me, and I can see she's very plainly hoping I'll say yes.

"I think that would be nice." I smile at her, and her shoulders relax.

"Thank you."

"Thank you for coming to talk to me." I laugh a little. "And I guess I need to thank my mom for getting ahold of you."

"She is quite the woman." Charlotte smiles sheepishly. "I'm not sure what persuaded me to listen to her. I tend to be overly suspicious of unknown callers."

"Mom has always been able to get things done." I shake my head admiringly.

"So, tell me. Is Malcolm due to come by today?"

With a sigh, I get up to make more coffee. "I have no idea. He's not made any appointments or been very official. He shows up, we fight, and then he leaves."

"Sounds productive," Charlotte says dryly.

Grimacing, I turn to face her. "And once Ronan kind of hit him."

Charlotte's mouth falls open. "What? Who hit him?"

"Ronan. He's . . . well, he's a friend, and he was here the day I confronted Malcolm about his lying."

"Ah." Charlotte nods knowingly. "And is this Ronan fellow part of the reason why you don't want to marry Malcolm?"

"You know what? You're nothing like how I imagined Malcolm's mother," I say instead of answering her question.

She laughs. "Yes, well, I've lived long enough to know there is a story behind everything."

"I assumed you'd, well, that you'd take Malcolm's side no matter what."

Her features settle back into the somber expression from earlier. "My dear, I love Malcolm with all my heart, but I love my granddaughter just as much. I hate that he hasn't told me about you or Poppy, and I can clearly understand how his actions have hurt you. His father is a good man, but he too has hurt me in the past with careless actions. Humans make mistakes. We all hurt those closest to us at some time or another. What remedies that is true repentance of wrongdoings. Unfortunately, Malcolm is not righting his wrong, and quite frankly, I am disappointed in his actions."

"I'm not exactly blameless either." I grimace. "I should have tried harder to find him after he transferred schools. I could have reached out to you."

She laughs. "I can see why you didn't. Did Malcolm tell you horror stories about me?"

"He did say you are very particular about your carpets, and if I ever came over, I couldn't wear shoes." I grin at her.

"I'll admit I abhor a dirty carpet." She winks good-naturedly. "I'm sure you could have done something, Cordelia, but there's no changing the past. What we can do now is attempt to heal what we can and to forgive. It's not easy, but we can't sit around and wish for a different past. I have to remind myself of that a lot. Especially now that I know the truth about Poppy's existence. I can't change how my son has acted, but I can hope he pulls himself together."

"I guess it's okay that Poppy has Malcolm's smile then," I say quietly. She raises an eyebrow, and I shrug. "I was a little jealous that Poppy looks anything like him after how he's acted, but the thing is, he looks like you. Which means my daughter looks like her grandma, who is a woman I'd be proud to have in my life."

Tears well in Charlotte's eyes, and she blinks hard. "I'm very glad I came."

"Me too." I laugh and wipe at my own eyes. "You've really helped."

Having finally finished her Cheerios, Poppy slaps her hands down onto her highchair, pulling our attention back to her. "Go-go! Mama, I Go-go?"

Charlotte straightens and smiles at Poppy. "Where do you want to go, my lamb?"

"Ah, no. She's asking for her goat. The one who almost ruined my shop." I point out the glass kitchen door.

"There's a goat?" Charlotte looks completely flummoxed.

I laugh. "Welcome to my life, Charlotte. There are goats, bees, and babies."

"Those aren't bad things to have in your life." She laughs.

"Yeah, well, wait until you meet the goat."

If someone had told me a year or even a week ago that I would have a better relationship with my daughter's grandmother than I would with her father, I would have laughed. Bad mothers-in-law are much more common than good ones. I'm not even married to Malcolm, yet his mother spent all day with us. She was excited about Poppy, interested in Go-go, and even wanted to talk about bees.

"How is she perfect and her son is . . . well, Malcolm?" I'm sitting at my kitchen table. Ronan is across from me, his legs stretched out under the table, where I'm using his shins as a footrest.

"Children aren't always a reflection of their parents, as strange as that is to think about. Did anyone else in his family show up?" He reaches across the table to take my hand, rubbing my knuckles with his thumb.

"No, just Charlotte. She said her husband is at some big convention in Wales."

"Imagine Wales having anything, much less a convention for biscuits," he mutters.

I ignore him and sip on my coffee-flavored milk. Ronan refuses to let me call what I drink coffee. He says it's degrading to the name of coffee. "My point is that I hope she sticks around."

Ronan pulls my hand up to his mouth to kiss. "And Malcolm?"

"What about Malcolm?"

"Do you hope he sticks around?" He fixes his eyes on me. Something is going on, but I can't quite tell what he's asking.

"I mean, I guess I can't stop him from being around his daughter, but I'm not going to start including him in everything. It would probably be good for Poppy to know him." I see something shift in Ronan's eyes. "But I don't want to get back together with him, if that's what you're asking."

His lips quirk behind his beard. "I wasn't sure—"

"Ronan." I lean toward him and use the hand he's just kissed to tug him closer by his beard. I gently place my mouth on his and kiss him slowly over my kitchen table. Pulling away just enough to speak, I whisper, "Do you really think I would give up kissing you?"

I feel him grin as he gives another kiss.

Chapter Seventeen
Ronan

I've reverted back to being sixteen. I can't remember the last time I spent every waking moment daydreaming about kissing someone. Then again, the last serious relationship I had was five years ago, and she didn't want to be with someone whose plans for life consisted of studying history and reading. Not that I blamed her. We weren't compatible, simple as that.

Cordy, on the other hand . . . well, she has pulled me into her world, and I plan to stay there forever. Who could give up catastrophic goats, bees, and an adorable baby?

The thought of Poppy makes me smile. She's one of the sweetest children I've ever met. Almost as much as I want to be with Cordy, I want to be present on Poppy's birthdays and Christmases. I want to take her to her first dance recital and be the too-proud Da in the aisle filming every twirl and off-key song.

Is it strange I'm ready to be a father? I'm nearly thirty, and a man has to settle down eventually, right?

There is a small chance that the reason I dislike Malcolm so much is I feel as though every child deserves a good father. I have a great one, but even as a child, I was well aware not everyone did.

Corwynn shuffles into the kitchen, breaking my train of thought. I spent the past half hour making coffee, and the rich smell seems to have lured my brother from his cave.

"What're you doing?" Corwynn grumbles as he slumps at his small kitchen table.

I deftly pour him a cup. I'm proud of my creation, as it did take me a solid ten minutes to locate any of Corwynn's measuring spoons. Good coffee must be measured well and accurately.

"I'm giving you coffee. Maybe it'll improve your sour mood." I place the cup in front of him and wait. After a moment, Corwynn takes a sip. His eyes widen a fraction, and I turn away, satisfied. Say what you will about how long it takes me to make coffee, it is always good when I set it in front of someone.

"So what's your plan, then?" Corwynn finally asks.

I pour myself a cup before coming to sit across from him. "My plan?"

"Yeah, well, you came here to talk me into going home, and now you've gone and found yourself a girlfriend. What's your plan, big brother? I hope you're not still thinking I'll go back home to take my exams, because I've moved on. I've got a life now."

I level Corwynn with a look that I hope reminds him of Da. "Why'd you leave, Cor?"

The question lands between us as Corwynn sips his coffee. Finally he says, "I don't know."

I open my mouth but then shut it.

Corwynn smirks a little at me. "I was tired of being at home, I guess. I like farming, but I don't want to take over Mam and Da's farm and have them hover over my shoulder. I want to have my own life with my own things. This seemed like a fine enough way to find my . . . independence."

"What does that have to do with your exams?" I frown at him. "You couldn't have waited until you finished school before becoming independent?"

He frowns back. "Do you know Mam hasn't shut up about how I need to finish with certain grades because you did?"

I pause. "So you didn't want to be compared to me?"

With a surly lift of a shoulder, he continues to frown. "Mam does that a lot. All I hear about is how you finished with top marks and look at you now. You're a professor and blah blah."

"You intentionally didn't finish school because Mam is proud of my academic achievements?" I snort. "That's the lamest excuse I've ever heard."

Corwynn goes beet red. "How'd you like it if she compared you to me all the time?"

"She does." I shrug, enjoying his baffled expression. "She calls me once a week and then tells me about how hard of a worker you are and how proud she is of your animal husbandry skills." I adopt a high voice that I think is a good likeness of Mam. "'Ronan, you were never very good with animals, but Corwynn has a magical touch. Did I tell you about the lamb he rescued? That boy is going to be a vet one day, and I couldn't be prouder. Why don't you get a dog or something?'"

Corwynn gapes at me. "She says that?"

"Of course she says that. Mams are always proud of their children. So what if she compares us sometimes? It could be worse. She could be comparing us to Siobhan."

At the mention of our cousin, Corwynn tips his head in acknowledgement of my statement. Siobhan graduated high school at fourteen, achieved her bachelor's degree at seventeen, and is currently working on her graduate degree. She has big plans to move to America and save the world after she achieves her master's. Talk about overachieving in life.

Corwynn's face scrunches up in thought. "Mam really thinks I could be a vet?"

"Well, you can hardly do it without proper schooling, but yeah, Mam reckons you'd be good at it. 'Tis a shame you decided you're going to stick it to me by not graduating." I shoot him a wink.

"I know what you're doing." He squints at me.

I take a sip of my coffee and let it fill my body with warmth. "Cor, the only thing I'm trying to do at this point is to show you I love you and that Mam loves you. I don't even care if you decide to stay here anymore. As long as you're content with where you are in life, and you stop shutting Mam out. She loves you very much. She wouldn't have sent me down here if she didn't."

I let him digest my words, and we both drink our coffee. The silence stretches so long that I think about Cordy again. What am I going to do with her? Ask her to marry me? That seems fast, as it's only been a couple of months. And then what? Have her move back to Ireland with me? Or do I stay here?

Corwynn breaks into my thoughts. "So you think I should become a vet?"

Coming back to the conversation, I shrug. "I think you should call Mam back."

"That's it? Don't you think I'd be good at it?"

"Well, why don't we ask Cheddar or any of the other animals that have somehow taken camp in this place," I say dryly.

For the first time since I arrived in Arbury, Corwynn grins. "The truth is, big brother, this place was overrun with rats when I moved in, and I've been trying to rid this place of them for weeks."

My jaw might have hit the table as I stare at him. "You're telling me you don't like having rats for roommates?"

Corwynn begins to laugh. "There is enough poison in this place to kill a horse."

"But you said it had a name!"

"Yeah, I wanted to get under your skin." Corwynn doubles over with laughter. "You should have seen the way you looked at me. Every time I saw you after I told you the rat's name was Cheddar, you stared at me with moon-eyes."

"Well, I thought you were training wild rats." I laugh.

"And I thought your only purpose of being here was to yell at me for bunking off the exams."

This sobers me, but not enough to stop a smile from spreading across my face. "What do you think now?"

"That Mam will have a fit when I tell her about the rats."

"So he's calling your mom?" Cordy briskly folds a hand-knitted scarf and pats her display of scarves, gloves, and sweaters.

"Yeah." I pause from chasing Poppy around the shop. "About time, too. Mam's been texting every day, asking if Corwynn's coming back." Poppy rushes at me, and I scoop her up and toss her gently into the air.

"Careful!" Cordy flinches as I catch a laughing Poppy.

"Aw, she loves it." I wink at her, but set Poppy down.

"I know . . ." Cordy's eyebrows furrow as she watches us. "I just worry about her hitting her head or you dropping her."

I lean in to give her a quick kiss on the forehead. "I promise to be very careful and to only toss her two inches into the air."

She rolls her eyes at me. "All right, then."

"Malcolm's not been back yet?"

"Well, Charlotte only came by yesterday. I expect she'll have to argue with Malcolm before he'll back off." Cordy sighs. "Vivian called earlier to tell me she can't get through to any of his superiors, so it's up to Charlotte whether or not my shop closes."

There's a scuffing sound as Poppy nearly falls over her own feet but catches herself. "Mama?" She makes a small motion with her hands. Cordy has been trying to teach Poppy sign language, which has utterly impressed me. I can barely speak English some days, and this one-year-old is already learning a second language.

"She's hungry." Cordy interprets for me.

"Thanks." I laugh and follow them into the kitchen.

I watch Cordy set Poppy up into her highchair and make a packet of oatmeal. "How is the honey going?"

"I need to check if I can harvest some today. I think I've come to the end of what I can get though. I'm waiting for Poppy's nap." Cordy blows on the oatmeal before setting it and a little plastic spoon in front of her grinning daughter.

"Can I help?"

She blinks at me. "You want to help?"

Well, since I don't know if I should quit my job and become a beekeeper to stay with you, might as well learn. "Sure."

Placing her hands on her hips, Cordy raises an eyebrow at me. "Ronan Thomson, you mean to tell me you've been willing to get close to bees the whole time and I'm just now finding out?"

"I'm only willing to get close to any kind of insect because of you, *mo mhuirnin*." She gives me a surprised look. "It means 'my dear.' I may as well start using my native tongue around you bilingual ladies."

She comes around the table to place a kiss on my cheek. "You should teach me some . . . is it Gaelic?"

"Yes, very good." I catch her hand and bring it to my mouth. "I warn you, I don't speak a lot of Gaelic on the regular, so I'm a bit rusty. Mam is great at it. She calls her sisters every Saturday, and they all chatter away like lost hens."

"I actually can't wait to meet your mom." She grins. "Meeting Charlotte was such a good experience, and I expect meeting your mom will be even better."

I ignore the rush of warmth associated with knowing Cordy wants to meet my family. She smiles at me, and the warmth intensifies. It takes all my willpower not to ask her to marry me right here. Instead, I say, "How are you liking the bees?"

Her smile widens. "Bees are pretty interesting little insects. Did you know you can influence the taste of honey by what plants the bees visit? That's why I'm trying to build up my herb garden. Rosemary honey or lavender honey would be amazing." She walks to the glass kitchen door and surveys her backyard.

"So the 'clover honey' labels mean something." I join her at the window. "That is pretty unique. I don't know if the grass that a cow eats matters to the taste of the milk."

"I think it's very human, in a way." Cordy watches her colorful hives. "We're influenced by what or who we surround ourselves with. It changes the way we act."

I squint at her. "You might be stretching that metaphor, love."

A full laugh escapes her, and she turns to me. "Well, you see what I'm saying."

"Yes, our actions are flavors of honey somehow."

Smacking my arm, she shakes her head. "I'm just saying certain plants influence the outcome of the bees' work. In the same way, different environments and people change the outcome of our behaviors too."

I fight to keep my face straight. "I still think you're stretching—"

With a groan, Cordy wraps her arms around me and lays her head on my chest. "I guess I'm trying to say that you've changed the outcome of my life. For the better, of course. You're the clover in my honey."

"That's the . . . sweetest thing anyone has ever said to me." I tickle her side. "Pun fully intended."

"Never mind then, Ronan," she laughs, swatting at me.

I pull her back against me. "No, no. I see what you're saying. It's a good comparison. Maybe not greeting card worthy, but—" I laugh as she pushes me away and rolls her eyes at me.

"To get back to your question, no, I don't need help today. Don't get me wrong, I'd love to have your company, but I only have one suit. We wouldn't want bees caught in your beard, now would we?" She makes more oatmeal, shooting me little grins as she adds some of the frozen raspberries she loves so much. The sight is so familiar, although so foreign at the same time, that I study it.

Maybe it's the flick of Cordy's princess-like hair or the way she measures the raspberries preciously before dumping an extra handful in, but something makes me want to keep this moment forever. At the same time, I want this to be my every morning. The thought of watching Cordy measure out frozen raspberries for the rest of my life is the most appealing thing in this moment.

"I think I'm going to marry you, Cordy Brown."

She blinks at me. "What?"

"I'm going to marry you." I watch her cheeks go pink. "Someday soon."

"Is this you asking?"

"No, I don't have a ring yet. I'm just letting you know that it's happening." I work to memorize the smile she shoots me. This morning has become one of my favorite memories already.

The rush of happy feelings that always hits me in Cordy's home motivates me to stand. I have to figure out if I can have this feeling for the rest of my life.

"Well, in the interest of protecting my beard from bees, I best be going." I give her a quick peck on her cheek.

"Do you have to talk to Corwynn?"

I haven't even told her yet about the great conversation my brother and I had this morning, but I give a noncommittal shrug. Let her think I'm hunting down Corwynn, when in reality, I'm finding her a ring.

Chapter Eighteen
Cordy

I take an extra second to look down at Poppy before I leave her room. She's already asleep, her eyelids heavy and her little round cheeks softening into her sleepy face.

If she were a plant that's flavored my life—I like my honey and plant analogy, even if Ronan doesn't—she'd be rosemary. It's not something you'd expect in honey, but it adds an explosion of flavor.

I lean against the doorframe of the room we share. My next project will be to set up her room. She's one now and could definitely benefit from having her own space. And I wouldn't hate to have my room back either. I never got to decorate a nursery for her. I've had visions of little girls' rooms for days now, and I blame Pinterest.

My little explosion of flavor. Okay, now I'm getting teary-eyed.

I swipe at my eyes and gently close the door. I need to harvest the remaining honey and straighten my shop. Before I can sweep away in my daily work, I take another second to thank . . .to thank who? God? The realization that I was about to thank God for Poppy startles me. And for Ronan and Charlotte. I don't think I've ever been tempted to thank God before.

"Well, look at that," I murmur as I grab my beekeeper's suit. Maybe I will join Barney at church someday. *Okay, Cordy, calm down. You're hardly going on a pilgrimage.*

Grinning, I dress in the beekeeper's suit. Barney would crack up at my trying to figure out what my knee-jerk impulse to thank God is about. I am thankful, though. For Poppy, Ronan, Vivian, Barney, Jack, my mom, Charlotte, and even Corwynn for stealing that farm job away. I would have been miserable, and a hay bale probably would have crushed me on my second day.

Pushing open the glass kitchen door, I tromp across the yard to my hives. It's pretty crazy how thankful I am for these insects too. And to think that I almost cried when they were dumped into my life.

"Well, God," I say to the sky, "If you plan on using my life as a catch-all dumping ground, I'm okay with that."

The door opens, and I glance up from straightening my remaining honey jars. The honey I just collected is waiting to be put through my extractor and isn't jarred yet. That will have to wait as I do need to keep my shop open as much as possible. Vivian and her mother have already come by to buy some dried herbs for a new focaccia bread Vivian is trying out. Vivian's mom chattered on about how she wishes I made beeswax candles, and I mentally jotted that down because it's a pretty good idea.

All the cheer from my previous two customers leaves me when I look up. My chest tightens as my eyes find Malcolm's pale face in the natural light of my shop. I scan his expression, trying to guess what his motivations for being here are. Am I about to lose my shop?

Malcolm clears his throat. "Cordelia, it's been . . . brought to my attention that I've treated you unfairly."

That's when I spot Charlotte standing in the doorway behind him, her arms folded across her chest. She's watching Malcolm with an intent gaze that tells me she dragged him here.

I shift and fold my arms across my chest as well, mirroring Charlotte. "Um, okay."

"I'm not going to shut down your shop. I'm sorry that I threatened to do so." He pauses for a second, then continues. "I wasn't thinking how this would impact Poppy, and the goat problem has been taken care of. I think." He glances past me toward the kitchen, as if he expects to see Go-go and Poppy playing a round of Go-Fish at my kitchen table.

"I appreciate your apology," I say solemnly.

He nods. "Good. I mean, I hope this is something we can move past."

"I'm sure we can."

"I don't want to get back together, though." Malcolm looks half apologetic, half horrified. I can't help the laugh that bubbles up in my chest.

"Oh, Malcolm," Charlotte scoffs. "Do you really think the poor girl would jump back into your arms after everything you put her through?"

He scowls at his mother. "I apologized, didn't I?"

Charlotte raises an eyebrow at him. "Yes, *after* your mother made you."

"Don't worry, Malcolm." I break the tension between mother and son. "I hadn't planned on asking you to marry me." Relief and irritation fight on his face, and I fight hard to not roll my eyes. "You don't want to marry me, and I don't want to marry you. It's a mutual feeling. No need to be upset that I'm not madly in love with you."

His shoulders relax a fraction of an inch. "That's fair, I suppose."

"Now, I don't know how you two plan to work this out"—Charlotte claps her hands once—"But I intend to be a part of my granddaughter's life as much as you'll let me." She turns hopefully toward me.

Something weird happens in my chest again. This whole situation with Malcolm has been awful. I spent days wondering if I would have to find a new home because of the apparent lack of jobs in this area. I wouldn't consider myself an anxious person, but Malcolm's presence put me on edge. But amidst all the confusion and worry, Poppy gained a grandmother.

"I would love to have Poppy's grandma around," I whisper past the lump in my throat.

"I've been thinking about that, actually. I'm not sure if I'm a 'grandma.'" Charlotte purses her lips. "How do we feel about me being called 'Gigi'?"

"That's similar to Go-go," I point out.

She frowns. "Ah, yes. What does your mother go by?"

"Nonna." I grin. "She said she used to call her grandma 'Nonna' and always loved it."

"Well, I'll think about it." Charlotte shakes her head and looks around the shop. "Where is my darling girl?"

"She's napping." I laugh. "But I do need to get her up."

Charlotte smiles around my little shop, her gaze finally landing back on Malcolm. "Oh, Malcolm, why do you look like you've eaten a pair of trousers? You should be glad of the fact that Cordelia accepted your half-hearted apology and hasn't kicked you out."

I can't help but wince a little at Charlotte's blunt words. True, Malcolm hasn't been very gracious, but then again, neither have I. There's still a hint of bruising around his left eye that reminds me of Ronan removing Malcolm the last time.

"I—" Malcolm scowls at the ground.

"Hang on, I'll get Poppy," I say, trying to break up the awkwardness.

As it turns out, Poppy is already awake. She grins up at me from where she's steadily kicking a crib slat. "Hi, Mama!"

"Hey, pretty girl." I scoop her up and blow a raspberry on her ankle. She squeals and pulls her foot away. I situate her on my hip and head back to the shop, but the sound of Malcolm practically spitting freezes me in the hall.

"How can we know that she's even my child?" His voice may as well be an angry wall keeping me from reentering the room.

"Malcolm," Charlotte hisses.

"Mother, we have no idea if Cordelia is lying—"

There's a smacking sound, and I wonder if Charlotte hit him. Chances are she hit one of the tables, but I'd rather imagine she smacked her son. "Malcolm, that girl is the spitting image of you as a baby. And I find Cordelia to be a kind person. I highly doubt she would lie—"

"When she comes asking for money—" Malcolm is once again interrupted, but this time by the door opening. There's a tense pause, and I realize this is my cue to enter as well. I set Poppy down and follow her back into the shop. There's never been a better ice breaker than a baby.

"There's my girl!" Charlotte falls to a knee and beams at Poppy, who grins back.

"Mother," Malcolm hisses, but Charlotte ignores him.

Then I see who is standing in the doorway. I open my mouth to greet Jack and Barney, but they're both frowning at Malcolm.

"Do you not believe our Cordy?" Barney's thin voice slices through the air. Malcolm blanches. When he doesn't say anything, Barney sighs and looks at me. "What are we to do about this young-un?"

I shake my head. "I don't know, Barney. I forgave him though, like you said I should." I shoot Malcolm a look that I hope conveys how he should also work on getting over whatever he has against me. To think that I used to dream about marrying this man-child.

"That's good, dear. I also said that forgiveness is not the same as reconciliation, do you remember?"

"I do." I keep my gaze on Malcolm. It's hard to see the man I used to love behind the anger and irritation. It's even harder to find love for him every time he talks about Poppy. A surge of anger pushes me to speak.

"Malcolm." His wide eyes fix on me. "If you're going to continue speaking about Poppy in a dismissive and hurtful way, I won't allow you around her. I would be happy if you wanted to be part of her life, but there would be clear lines drawn. And I don't expect you to make a decision right now."

If there's ever a medal for maturity, I should be getting a letter in the mail tomorrow informing me of my win.

Malcolm does a great impression of a goldfish for a moment. "I'll think about it."

That's all I can expect, I suppose. I want to add that he has to stop saying Poppy isn't his, but I think that was implied. At least, I hope.

Jack claps his hands. "Looks like there won't be a need for me to break out the old men after all." He pats his biceps, and I giggle. He shoots me a mock hurt look but then winks. "Oh, and Cordy, your fella asked if you'd meet him outside."

Chapter Nineteen
Cordy

My heart does an excited two-step at the mention of Ronan. At least, I hope that's who "my fella" is.

"In that case," Malcolm says briskly. "I'll be taking my leave." He gestures to Charlotte, and she reluctantly hands me Poppy and follows her son. As they reach the door, Malcolm turns back around, not meeting my eyes. "Cordelia. I would like to be aware of major events in Poppy's life. Please," he adds as a last-minute thought.

It takes a lot not to quip that his showing back up is a major event. Instead, I nod. "I can do that."

Malcolm leads the way out, followed by his mother and then by a beaming Barney and Jack. Jack even shoots me one last wink before he disappears. I snuggle Poppy close for a second. I want to give my guests enough time to leave. I generally prefer life without spectators.

Stepping outside, I close the door behind myself. As much as I love Barney, Jack, and even Charlotte, I don't need them—or Malcolm—staring at me while I talk to Ronan.

I'm surprised to find Ronan in my front yard, holding Go-go. Okay. What is happening? For a moment, I thought Ronan might be, I don't know, proposing or something from the way everyone was acting, but this doesn't look like a proposal to me.

"Did she get out?" I look at Go-go chewing her cud in Ronan's arms. There's a sprig of lavender tucked into her collar for some reason.

"Ah." Ronan shifts nervously. "No. I was sort of trying to reenact our first meeting."

Wait, *is* he proposing?

A flood of emotions zips through my body. Do I want to marry him? What kind of question is that? Of course I want to marry him. But is it too early? I don't want to rush anything, especially not with Poppy. Okay, the best solution is to just see what he's asking. I fight to keep my face calm and wait for Ronan to continue.

He sets Go-go down, and the little goat cheerfully makes her way over to me and jumps up to try to nibble Poppy's toes. Poppy squirms and giggles. Without taking my eyes off Ronan, I gently place Poppy in the grass, and she begins petting Go-go.

"I . . . I wanted to do this well," he finally says, and I frown in confusion.

"Do what well?"

Ronan shakes his head. "I didn't realize Barney and Jack were here. And Malcolm." He frowns slightly.

I place my hands on my hips. "Ronan, what's going on? Why does it matter if anyone was here? They're gone now." I scan the empty street.

This is starting to sound less and less like a proposal and more and more like a bad news kind of thing. My heart flinches at the idea of this being bad news. Is he dying? Am I dying? *Wait. What?* I give my head a quick shake to get rid of the ridiculous thoughts.

"I'm trying to ask you to be my wife, Cordy, but I didn't . . . I wanted it to be private and even sweet, and now"—he gestures at Go-go, who is steadily nibbling his pant leg—"I'm wondering what I was thinking, because you deserve so much more—"

I cut off his monologue by stepping forward, grabbing his face, and kissing him. Turns out I don't need to think about the answer. Go-go headbutts my shin gently and bounces away.

Ronan pulls away and looks down at me. "Did that goat headbutt you?"

"Yes, I will marry you."

"What? But I haven't . . . I haven't even properly asked."

I laugh at his expression. "Do you want me to say no?"

"No." He runs a hand through his hair and sighs. "You deserve a better proposal. Not one with a goat headbutting you. I don't know what I was thinking. I got nervous."

I scoop up Poppy, who has abandoned trying to get Go-go to hold still. "Why would you be nervous?"

"You wanted to take things slow." He hitches one shoulder up. "I'm normally so much better at these things."

I raise an eyebrow at him. "Oh, yeah? Have you proposed to a lot of girls then?"

He snorts. "No. But I usually think out a plan before I go trying to execute it."

"Since the moment I got here, my life hasn't gone as planned. I didn't plan on bees or a goat, or you. I think it's Arbury that makes everything a little unique. I like it that way." I grin and then kiss Poppy on the head. "It seems very fitting that you'd propose to me with a goat. I'm surprised you didn't figure out how to incorporate the bees somehow."

"I thought about tying the ring to a bee." He grins. Then with a startled look, adds, "The ring! I never gave you the ring."

He takes a small black velvet box from his pocket, but before he opens it, he pauses. I can't help the laugh that bubbles up when he makes a slow descent to one knee. Grinning, he holds out the box. "Will you be my wife, Cordy Brown?"

A delicate ring with a teardrop-shaped pearl stares back at me. Three diamonds sit on either side of the pearl, tiny sparkly bodyguards. The ring isn't alone, and a small necklace with a matching pearl pendant is snuggled around it.

Ronan continues, "And Poppy, can I be your daddy to protect and love you? The necklace is for you if you say yes."

It's then that I realize I'm crying. It's closer to sobbing, really. There were times back when it was just me and Poppy in our cramped little apartment when I wondered what a moment like this would be like. Would Poppy be remembered? And here is Ronan, kneeling in front of me, not only having tried to make this a cute, memorable proposal, but also including my little girl. The fact that she is remembered and will be cared for by this man would make anyone cry.

"I think we both say yes," I whisper, trying to slow the tears. "On the condition that we plan the wedding for a year so my mom doesn't have a heart attack over how quickly we got married."

He grins. "My mam would appreciate that too."

"And . . . well, where are we going to live?"

"I've always liked the idea of keeping bees." Ronan winks and I throw my arms around him the best I can while still holding my daughter.

Poppy takes this moment to grab Ronan in her own mini bear hug. "Up?"

Ronan shoots me a glance. "I'll toss you up if your mam is okay with it."

Laughing, I step back and let Poppy cling to him like a baby koala. I take the little jewelry box from Ronan with a wink. "I guess just this once."

He leans in and kisses my cheek. "I promise to keep you both safe. You've made me a very happy man, Cordy."

I wipe my leaking eyes and beam back at him. Poppy kicks her legs. "Up!"

Ronan lifts Poppy, and she squeals. I watch them and clutch Ronan's promise to my chest. *Things really are looking up, Pops.*

Ronan

SHE SAID YES!

Epilogue
Cordy – Five years later

"Mama." Poppy wheels into the kitchen. With a clomping of hooves, Go-go follows her in.

"What's up, sweets?" I finish tying off a bundle of lavender. Its sweet aroma relaxes me, which is something I desperately need. My back may actually collapse if this baby doesn't come soon.

"Can Go-go come to the hospital when the baby is born?" Poppy skips to my side and picks up a small sprig of lavender.

"Well, baby, I don't think they allow full-grown goats into the hospital. Especially goats who are pregnant with twins and due any day."

"Why not?" Poppy shrugs. "She's pregnant, you're pregnant. Everyone's pregnant."

"She's got a point," Ronan calls from the living room.

"Oh, hush," I shout back. "We're not bringing a goat to the hospital, end of story."

"How are we going to manage Corwynn's graduation? That's in two weeks." Ronan pokes his head into the kitchen.

I shrug. "I figured we'd drive up and stay with your parents."

"Cordy, I'm not taking you and our newborn son to a sheep farm. What about germs?" Ronan frowns down at me. "I'll just have to tell Corwynn we can't come."

"You and Poppy can go."

"And leave you here with Callum by yourself?"

I wave at Ronan, trying to appear confident rather than dismissive. "I've handled a newborn by myself before, honey. Plus, Mom will be in, remember? Her plane comes in tomorrow. And you can't miss Corwynn's graduation. You're pretty much the reason he became a vet anyway."

I can see on Ronan's face the desire to be a supportive brother wrestling with the need to be with me. Finally, he sighs. "All right, but only because your mam will be in. My mam will have a fit that she won't get extra time with Callum, though."

"She's always welcome here." I return to my lavender sprigs.

Warmth and the smell of leather envelops me as Ronan wraps his arms around me from behind. "Everyone is welcome around you. You make everything feel like home."

I turn to kiss him. Poppy makes an exaggerated gagging sound but then grins. Snuggling into his arms, I smile as Ronan caresses my very round stomach. *I swear this baby is going to weigh nine pounds.* Callum kicks at his daddy's touch, and Ronan chuckles.

"He'll be a footie player if we're not careful." He kisses my head. "You've given me a good life, Cordy Thomson."

It may have been nearly four years since we got married, but I still love it when he uses my "new" name. I laugh a little. "Well, that's no small feat."

"You're right, it's not." He winks at me, and I roll my eyes.

"So when does your paternity leave go into effect?"

When Ronan told his boss at the university that he was planning on marrying a girl in southern England and staying in the countryside, I expected them to graciously let him go. Instead, his boss asked if he would teach online classes and one in-person class each summer. Ronan jumped at the idea, and now he works remotely from home. He still gets an amazing paternity package, which is helpful, because I'm not sure how much I'll be able to do right after Callum makes his appearance.

"Next week."

"That should be enough time." I mentally check off Ronan from my getting-ready-for-another-baby list. A wave of happiness and nerves washes over me. "We're having a baby."

"*Another* baby, you mean," Poppy yells from the other room.

"You'll always be my baby," I shout back.

"And mine too," Ronan adds. "I still remember throwing you up in the air while your mam watched on in horror, afraid I'd drop you."

"It's not safe," I mumble. I'm cut off from more grousing by a knock on the door and Poppy's shout of "Glam!"

"Charlotte's here." I make to get out of my chair, but Ronan flaps his hands at me to wait.

"You'd better not be getting up, Cordy," Charlotte shouts through the house. She started calling me Cordy pretty soon after Malcolm and I parted ways, but she still somehow manages to make my name sound high-society in her posh accent.

"I'm not an invalid," I cry and push my chair back. "I can still stand—"

I'm cut off by a familiar sensation. It's not the kind of thing you forget, no matter how long it's been. Ronan sees my face and immediately comes toward me. "What? What is it?"

"My water just broke."

"What?" Charlotte barrels into the kitchen.

"Good timing, Glammy," I say, grinning at her.

"What are you waiting for? Go!" Charlotte ushers me toward the door.

"Oh, Charlotte, I'm not even having contractions." I move around her and slowly to the sink to grab a towel. "We could probably even make it to service tonight." I say this mostly to watch Charlotte's and Ronan's reactions. They don't disappoint.

"Cordy—" Ronan starts, his eyes the size of saucers.

"Tonight's Barney's night to sing." Barney has been practicing his solo for weeks, and I've been looking forward to hearing him. I had no idea that Barney was so involved with the music at the little church in the center of town.

"Barney will understand that you're *giving birth*," Ronan says. "I'm grabbing your hospital bag."

He hurries from the room, and I grin at Charlotte. She shakes her head at me. "You're not funny."

I laugh. "I think I'm pretty funny. Anyway, maybe you could take Poppy to church?"

Charlotte nods. "I will, but I'll also have my phone on the loudest setting because I don't want to miss anything. You better call your mother."

I groan. "I have plenty of time—"

"We're having a baby!" An excited-but-nervous Ronan appears in the doorway again. "I called your mam, and the bags are in the car. Are you ready?"

Tears prick my eyes. Stupid pregnancy hormones.

Ronan's face crumples in concern. "Why are you crying? Does it hurt?"

"No." I laugh a little. "I'm just really happy." I pull him in for a kiss. "We're having a baby."

"And we should go." Ronan scoops me up, and I smack his arm.

"I can walk!" Although it is kind of nice to be carried as if I'm not forty pounds heavier than I was nine months ago. Ronan pauses long enough for me to kiss Poppy and tell her to be good for her Glam before hurrying out the door.

He stops beside the car and gently places me down. "I worry about you. I promised to protect you, remember?"

I lean up and kiss him. "And you've made good on that promise every day since I met you. Now let's go have this baby."

The car skids a little in Ronan's rush to get onto the road, and I take a moment to look back at my cute little cottage home. It's come a long way since Poppy and I first moved in. We all have. I look over at the man sweating while he drives and smile. I guess this all was meant to . . . bee.

Thanks for reading!

Please leave a review and let me know what you thought!

Reviews are extremely helpful for authors, so thank you for taking the time to support me and my work.

Acknowledgments

This book would not be here without the support and talent of so many people. I could not have done this alone (or at least it wouldn't have been done very well). It wasn't simply human talent that brought Meant to Bee to mind either. I truly feel as though God has placed this story on my heart and now into your hands for a reason. Each time that I wondered where this story was going and how I could incorporate Truth into it, He provided answers. I can never praise Him enough for that.

I am also thankful to:

Michael, my sweet husband—You have listened to me ramble about this book for over a year and have always been kind, encouraging, and loving. Thank you for understanding that my head is always in the clouds and for being my biggest supporter. I love you and I'm beyond blessed that God has brought us together.

Violet Rose, my daughter—Thank you for taking naps. Thank you even more for your love and kisses. I hope that one day you'll love books even more than I do.

Mom and Dad—Thank you for seeing the potential of storytelling in me as a child and pushing me to follow my gift. It may have taken twenty years, but I'm finally taking writing seriously! Also, a special thanks to Dad for his insight on beekeeping.

My siblings and their loved ones—Thank you for supporting me via love and buying me more books for "research."

Mommy Writers—You ladies have motivated and cheered me on since I met you. I can't thank you all enough for lifting me up on days when momming is just as hard as writing.

My wonderful beta readers—You have made this story a thousand times better with your kind and helpful comments.

Kelsey Gietl, my cover designer—Thank you for giving Meant to Bee such a beautiful cover to enter the world in.

Heather Wood, my editor—Thank you for putting up with my parentheses and for making this story so clean.

Gail Sears—Thank you for asking me if I'll remember you when I'm famous like Mark Twain. I'll never forget you (I couldn't even if I tried!).

Kylie Hunt, Bethany Cox, Tiffany Davis, Christine Boatwright, Latisha Sexton, Sarah Everest, Sara Whitley, B.M. Baker, M.J. Padgett, Candice Howard, Jennifer Hunt, Cady Comeaux, Jordan Comeaux, Candice Yamnitz, Cleopatra Margot, and Eliza Noel—Thank you for your (virtual) friendship, encouragement, and tips.

My friends who have simply been there, cheering me on—Thank you. I couldn't have done this without you.

Readers—It is still surreal that there are those of you who want to read something I've written. You are huge blessings in my life. Thank you for spreading the word about this story.

ABOUT THE AUTHOR

Storm Shultz is an author of Christian and Inspirational fiction. She has always enjoyed storytelling, but didn't take writing seriously until 2020, shortly after her oldest child was born. Storm lives with her pastor husband and children in rural Kentucky. She loves reading, baking, and thinking about fictional people.

Connect with Storm:
Website: www.stormshultz.com
Instagram: @takingbooksbystorm
Facebook: @stormshultzauthor
Twitter: @stormshultz

Sign up for the monthly newsletter

to receive a free ebook (Yvette's Moon – a retelling of Jael), giveaways, bonus content, and updates from the author.

www.stormshultz.com

Made in the USA
Las Vegas, NV
25 January 2023